One Story One Blunder One Destiny

Mehul Jain

Mystic Panda

*To the woman who is the reason for my existence,
survival and everything that I am today, thank you...*

Contents

Chapter 1

Introduction

We were sitting in the waiting area reserved for the spirits who departed from their bodies. It is a small area in a hollow space overlooking earth on one side and those beautiful rings of Saturn on the other. A platform that defies laws of gravity. After realizing it is for departed spirits, we had come to terms with how the place is nothing like you know a place should be.

We were waiting here while our records are being pulled out to know the next role we play in the universe. As they have enshrined it in Bhagwad Gita,

'Never the spirit was born; the spirit shall cease to be never;'

or simply put, the spirit never dies, it changes forms, and with every new form comes a new role, just like a new job or promotion, or based on your karma, demotion, if you deserve.

Ohh yes! we are here because we have been released from our bodies, they gave us in our form as humans on earth. The last thing I remember is I had met with an accident on my way to school where I used to teach. There was a hailstorm; I lost control of the car and banged into a tree on the corner of the road and the next thing I know is I am here.

This usually chaotic reception at the crossroads of the multiverse was unusually empty today. A passerby mentioned that it was that time of the year where the caretakers of various universes in the multiverse play against each other. The winner takes home the prestigious title of champions they hold for the next 4 years. It was called 'Olympics of the Titans'.

We look around to see two other people just like us waiting for their deeds to be processed on the 'judgment day' as written in the Bible. Also, there is an oddly looking old man with a white beard that had grown up to his knee. He was wearing a white cloak that looked like he had pulled out a cloud and wrapped it around himself.

As most of us were still trying to comprehend what was happening around, the old man approaches us. He then says in a heavy voice, "It might take some time while your deeds are being processed. Since there is nothing better to do while you wait, let me tell you a story which I would never forget. This is a story from the time when I was the caretaker of your precious little home, Earth."

Chapter 2

The Beginning...

Ishan woke up that morning when the alarm bell rang. Just like all other days, he drank tea from the cup that was placed on the side table by Priya Didi and got ready for work. But the day was nothing like any other day for Ishan. It was a big day for him at work. Anyone who knew him little could have sensed the nervousness that was breeding over his excitement. For Priya Didi in whose shelter he had grown, it would not be difficult. She asked Ishan the reason for this excitement with some hand gestures which Ishan could understand in seconds.

Priya Didi was a 38-year-old woman who had come to Ishan's house as a maid about 19 years ago when Ishan was just 10. During Ishan's growing up days, Priya Didi took care of most of Ishan's chores. From picking and dropping him off to school and his football practice, dance, or swimming class to helping him in craft, it covered all. For Ishan, Priya Didi was like an elder sister he never had. Priya also treated Ishan like a little brother she had to leave behind on getting married and moving to Mumbai to start a new life. Soon after coming to Mumbai, Priya Didi had joined as a maid to Ishan's house.

A few years after Priya Didi came to Mumbai, she suffered an accident. It happened when she was going to the market to buy some groceries for Ishan's house. A bull that went loose in the neighborhood picked her up by the horns and threw her away, only to land on her skull. This caused an irreparable damage to her hearing abilities.

After spending a few months in the hospital and at her home where she stayed with her husband, for recovery, Priya Didi was back to Ishan's house as their housemaid and his elder sister. While Priya was in the hospital, Ishan's family had funded her treatment and every other help and support she needed. She was family to them. But one thing they couldn't do for her was to make her talk and hear again. As Priya Didi was not disabled by birth, it was harder for her to adapt to the new way of living.

Ishan was now 28 and a Senior Executive at Sirius Saviors. It was a technology company he had been working for over 6 years since the time they hired him from the campus of the premier technology institute of India. At Sirius, Ishan along with another colleague Ayush had been working on a project for developing an application that could change the way people communicated, especially the disabled. It was an application that could hear the words spoken and convert the same into sign language for people with hearing disabilities. On the other hand, it converted the sign language used by people with speaking disabilities into words for others to understand. The project they had named 'Enabler' after what it really did.

Ishan had conceptualized the idea in affection for Priya Didi and his firsthand experience of troubles in communication for people with speaking and hearing disabilities like Priya Didi.

Sirius had internally cleared the project after all the testing and trials gave exceptional results. Today, the top management was going to meet and decide on whether the project could be commercialized and taken to the market. That's what all the excitement and nervousness for Ishan was about.

Ishan reached the office a little earlier than usual that day as staying at home made him more anxious. Ayush was feeling the same and therefore, he reached early too. All the anxiousness within could not let their hands press the keys of the laptop without trembling. So they decided to just loiter around in the cafeteria instead of pretending to work.

"Should we not be inside the room in case they needed some questions to be addressed?" Ayush broke the silence and asked Ishan.

Ishan flustered and said nothing and nodded in agreement.

Ishan sat at the table and started biting his nails. Ayush was fidgeting with a crystal ball from his desk, which if would have fallen off his hands could create a dent on the floor.

Ayush and Ishan were very excited about the project. It was the project they were working on for more than 4 years now. In the process, they had met several people with disabilities and people associated with them to understand the issues they face. With all these interactions, they had grown very close to the cause. Therefore, they thought of the project more as a philanthropic effort to help those in need than a business opportunity to succeed.

Ishan's desk phone rang. Calming his nerves, he answered. It was their boss on the line who said, "We got a go ahead. We are launching the application in the upcoming TechCon India (India chapter of world's largest technology conference) with the name 'Enabler'."

Ishan smiled so widely, making it look like a 180-degree curve on his face, and said, "Thank you", while nodding to Ayush hinting at the approval from the board. They jumped off their chairs and hugged each other. It was a turning point for their careers. Their first project was going to be out in the market.

The day had arrived; the stage was set; suits were ready, and the speeches were written. As Ishan and Ayush walked on to the stage to unveil their creation, the crowd applauded in hope and aspiration.

As communication has been the biggest barrier for life and livelihood of those with hearing and speaking disabilities, it was one of the path breaking ideas. The success of this product was going to probably change the future of the disables or so they felt.

The 30 minutes presentation from Ishan and Ayush, where Ishan spoke the most, was filled with tech jargon which for the ones present was bliss and for us little to understand. Almost every major tech industry pioneer, leader, and enthusiast attended TechCon India. Some of the foreign tech experts also attended the conference to represent a global interest in India's technology industry.

After the presentation, as Ayush and Ishan walked around, several people came forward to appreciate their work. It was not just the startup geeks and enthusiasts that were impressed; they impressed some industry leaders too. Enabler was not just considered a good technology; it was also considered as a step forward towards technology that aids humans. More than a technological breakthrough, it was something that furthers the entire purpose with which they originally introduced technology to humankind, aid humans, and make their lives better.

Enabler had received a very good response at the 3 days TechCon in India. It was tried by various attendees, including those representing the user community. This added more weight to the confidence Ayush and Ishan already had. Sirius was also very confident about the success of the application.

Therefore, they allotted a significant portion of their operational and marketing budget for this project. They wanted to add more Indian languages to their application for users from the rest of the country. Also, sign language was different across the world and therefore along with voice language, a lot of incremental work was needed for a global launch.

With the initial success of Enabler in the Indian market, Ishan proposed that they should launch Enabler in the International market. To start with, Sirius should first launch the product in TechCon Europe and the TechCon US scheduled for the coming month, he proposed.

Sirius's management agreed.

To cover larger ground, Sirius decided to split responsibilities between Ishan and Ayush. Ishan was told to go for the product launch in TechCon Europe to be held in Austria next month to reach the European audience. Ayush was asked to launch the product in the US to cover the North American region. As the product launch was just a month away, technology and field teams started working tirelessly. They had to add various European languages to the application for it to be relevant for the market., At the same time, Ishan and Ayush were preparing their presentations for the largest event they had ever been a part of, rather largest audience they had ever addressed.

Ishan headed to Austria for his presentation for the European market and Ayush was to leave next week for his presentation in the US. After the conference, Ishan had to go to the UK and meet some potential partners for collaboration opportunities to spread the usage of the products in corporate offices.

The day had arrived, Ishan was on a 1,500 square feet stage, which was 15 feet high above the ground. Ishan felt like he was standing in a stadium with the world watching him over. The first row of people was so far away from him that through the lights that were showered on him from the front and the sides, he could hardly see who they were. As he walked on the stage, he could not feel the ground and felt he was made to levitate. After a deep breath, he uttered the first words and fumbled. It wasn't the start he ever imagined getting at this stage. But then, that was the last time he feared that stage. He took another deep breath and continued with his presentation. From that point on, the presentation was flawless and amazed everyone in the audience.

By the end, with the response he got from the audience, it was clear that the launch had created the buzz they hoped for. They got some interest in partnerships on the first day of the conference itself and Ishan was asked to visit their office in the UK later that week. The trip to UK was anyway a part of the plan and therefore, Ishan extended it by a few more days to take care of the growing interest on the ground.

Chapter 3

Almost Found The One…

With the successful launch of Enabler in the European market at Ishan's hands, the eyes were on Ayush to make the launch successful in the US market. Ayush left for the US with a lot of pressure, preparation, and hope. Ayush reached New York, where TechCon was to be held, 3 days before the day he was scheduled to take the stage. However, the next day, he got a call from India.

It was from his mother. She said, "Ayush, papa has met with an accident, you have to come back immediately."

From the moment of excitement to take the biggest stage of his life, he was in dismay. Ayush asked, "What happened", but his mother couldn't stop crying.

Ayush's uncle took the phone and said, "It was a hit and run, come here as soon as possible."

Hearing his mother cry, and the way his uncle

spoke to him, he knew it was serious, an image of it being terminal was hovering over him.

Ayush scrambled and ensured that he got a flight back the same day. The launch in the US market in the TechCon was very important to Sirius and with clouds of uncertainty over the launch of Enabler in the US in the absence of Ayush, the presence of Ishan in the UK came to rescue of Sirius. Thanks to the extended trip to the UK, Ishan was able to fill in for Ayush. Ishan immediately took the flight to New York where the TechCon was being hosted and Ishan reached the venue just in time for the presentation, rushing to the podium directly from the airport. With his experience in Austria, there was no doubt that the presentation would go very smoothly, and so it did. It felt almost like the repeat of Austria in New York for Ishan.

Later that day it was the gala dinner for all the TechCon participants to network. Ishan was not very keen on going as he was tired after the long and tiring trip which started from Austria almost ten days ago. However, the success of the presentation would only be known by interacting with people and gauging their interest in partnerships, therefore he went to the gala dinner, anyway.

That evening would not be an ordinary evening

for Ishan, and he would know about it as the evening unfolds. Ishan reached there early. He thought he would leave early from the gala dinner and give himself some rest but that wasn't the plan for him. As he was walking around talking to executives from the tech industry including some of the tech moguls who had graced the occasions with their presence, everyone was heaps and praises for their creation and how Ishan and Ayush, who was missing all the limelight, are going to be not just the game changers for Sirius but also for the community with hearing and speaking disabilities, with Enabler.

Sheena, a 26-year-old technology student, had also made it to the event uninvited. Uninvited may not be accurate, she got an invitation by misrepresenting herself as a news reporter. Actually, it was not an absolute misrepresentation as she had a tech blog with around a hundred followers diligently following her weekly newsletter, most of whom were her college mates. She wanted to be part of the event to network, learn more about new technology and get some insights to make her tech blog go viral. As Sheena was walking around in an elegant grey gown with a 4-inch heel beneath, making her look like a perfect fit for modeling, she saw Ishan talking to people. Ishan was wearing a black suit with shoes that were so shiny that you could see light reflecting from it. Sheena had heard how Ishan's presentation was considered as being path breaking in the industry and how philanthropic, in a sense, the idea was. With a hope to get some content from him that could go viral, amongst her followers which represented a chunk of the Indian diaspora, she walked towards Ishan to talk to him. As Ishan laid his first sight on her, something within him sparked. It was the feeling that sends your entire body numb for a second and the blood rushes through all your body at godspeed at the next moment. As Sheena said "Hi" and extended her hand to greet Ishan, he paused and smiled, hiding the jaw drop and heart eyes behind it.

"Hi, hi", Ishan responded with a soft handshake and a gleaming smile.

Sheena added, "You were good on stage and the application looks fantastic too. I am glad technology is being used for the right purpose again."

With no change in the smile and still holding Sheena's hand, Ishan said, "Thanks you, thank you!"

Sheena smiled and flinched from the handshake that should have been over a while ago. As Ishan realized he was still holding Sheena's hand, he said, "Ohh, sorry" and snapped away.

After a few seconds of awkward silence, where Ishan stared at Sheena as if he had never seen a woman so beautiful, Sheena asked, "So why and how did you get this idea for Enabler?"

After taking a few seconds to focus on the words and not Sheena's face, Ishan replied, "It was someone in my family who inspired me."

"So, you have a nag to help people around you," Sheena said.

Ishan replied, "If I can, what could be any better."

The conversation went on and on and it was mostly all about Sheena asking and Ishan responding.

Ishan was in his late twenties with a charming, composed personality. Sheena was in her mid-twenties with a geeky, nerdy attitude with an adventurous touch to it, not quite how Ishan led his life. Except for the meeting of two people interested in technology, it was the meeting of two opposites but not quite the opposite to not like each other. As the night progressed, they spoke more and more about things that didn't matter or at least matter to the occasion they met for. Things that were absolutely unrelated to what they were there for. Neither did they talk about what Sheena did or where she was from, except that she was studying at MIT to graduate next year and post which she would move back to India where she planned to have her own startup for which various ideas were just seeding in her mind.

At one point into their conversation, when Ishan almost dropped a glass of wine, spilling it all over the table while trying to make a hand gesture, they realized they were a little tipsy. Being amongst nerds, including some of the industry tycoons, they realized it was not the best place to lose themselves in alcohol, and therefore, they headed out and hit a restaurant to eat something. The night, that was full of laughs and giggles, seemed like it was not meant to give in to sunrise today.

In the middle of everything, the night which seemed to never end, Sheena abruptly said, "Oh my god, it's too late, I should head back to my hotel, I have a flight to catch tomorrow morning to Cambridge."

Ishan wanted to tell Sheena so many things, he wanted to ask her to wait or drop her at the hotel. At that moment, Ishan also thought of asking Sheena for her number but held back with a thought, "she would have had asked if she wanted to." After all these inner thoughts of wanting to communicate with Sheena on the continuity of today, he just said, "Ohh Okay, you better get going soon then. Let me call for the check."

Sheena left that day, and all she left with Ishan were some beautiful memories and her first name. On the way back to his hotel room, Ishan was only thinking about Sheena, a tech geek who was as mature as a person in his mid-twenties could get and as maverick as Ishan would want his partner to be. Sheena was the perfect blend of a girl Ishan always had in mind.

Chapter 4

Ayush's Journey...

Once Ayush was back from the US, he rushed to the hospital where his father was battling for his life. With every passing minute the chances of his survival were getting grim. The doctors had already told them that there was very little they could do about Ayush's dad's recovery since significant damage had been done to his organs and recovery was difficult due to his age. Ayush scrambled every resource he could to figure out how his father could be saved, but to his disappointment, nothing seemed to work.

That night when he was sitting beside his father's bed watching over him. While trying to get some sleep, he saw a bright light flashing on the other side of his father's bed and disappear in a fraction of a second. He thought he was hallucinating because of lack of sleep. On the next morning, he got up, holding his father's fingers which he didn't remember holding at any point last night. As he moved and turned to see his father, he saw his eyes blinking. He rubbed his own eyes to see it again. They were still blinking. Ayush's father had gained consciousness after four days. He couldn't believe it and rushed to get the doctor and the nurse on duty. The nurse came in and checked the beeping monitors, his father's pulse and temperature. She was in disbelief and called the doctor. The doctor also came and checked the same beeping monitor and the pulse and looked at Ayush and smiled. The doctor told him that his father was recovering, and that he should be fine.

Ayush was happier than ever before. He called home to inform his mother, but she didn't answer the call. It was early in the morning, just past dawn, and so he thought his mother would be sleeping. He had asked the nurse to watch over his dad while he visits home, which was just within a walking distance. Instead of ringing the bell and wake his mother up from the sleep she desperately required after so many sleepless nights, he opened the door with the keys he had. Ayush saw her sleeping on the bed with peace and therefore went for a shower first, instead of waking her up. After the shower, he went to wake her up. As he touched her, he felt her senseless body, saw her face that looked a little pale. She was dead. The doctor who came home on Ayush's call confirmed that she died in her sleep with a heartache. He thought today he was the bearer of good news, only to know otherwise.

∞ ∞ ∞

After a few months, Ayush's dad had fully recovered, and Ayush was back to work at Sirius. At Sirius, however, Ayush had lost his importance, or at least so he felt. With Ishan being made the face of Sirius in the international market and Ayush being sidelined for just being not around for a few months while Sirius was having the steepest growth, the relationship between the two started becoming sour. As much as he was a friend of Ishan since much before the time they started working on Enabler together and making it success ready, the lack of recognition to Ayush at the hands of Ishan, or so it appeared to Ayush, led to a feud between the two. After a few weeks of experiencing this treatment, Ayush was in an argument with Ishan.

"How does it feel to be kept at a pedestal?" Ayush asked Ishan while waiting for his coffee at the office cafeteria.

Ishan was taken aback by the tone of Ayush. It would be wrong to say that he did not notice the change in Ayush's behavior since he was back in the office, but he thought Ayush was just trying to cope with the recent personal tragedies he had to face. Ishan, therefore, took Ayush's edgy tone as sarcasm and let the comment slide through him without any tipping reaction.

Ayush continued to add, "How does it feel to be the sole reason for the success of Sirius?", almost instigating Ishan with his sarcasm.

Ishan then replied, "We are the reason for its success, we did it together."

Ayush took them as the words of pity that Ishan was using for him and said, "Did we? Doesn't look like with all the promotions and importance you are receiving...."

"What do you mean?" Ishan asked.

Ayush said, "You know what I mean. You consciously sidelined me when I was struggling personally. You used it as an opportunity to make me irrelevant in the entire scheme of things."

Ishan said, "You are getting it all wrong. We didn't bother you, as you were taking care of your father. It felt wrong."

Ayush replied, "Ohh, don't give me that crap of yours. You consciously kept me out of it so that you could take all the credit."

After this spat between the two, Ayush quit his job at Sirius and almost a decade of friendship between the two came to an abrupt end. After quitting Sirius, Ayush joined the product development team of Alpha-Net in India. The product development team of Alpha-Net was the size of all of Sirius's operations. Ayush was like one laborer tasked with a job and making small codes or undertaking code testing or undertaking code integration jobs. Ayush had no big role to play at Alpha-Net of his own in stark contrast to what he was meant to achieve and almost did at Sirius.

Ayush, while working at Alpha-Net, was looking for a pet project to work on, a little something of his own. In his pursuit of an idea to solve something with technology and make a difference in the life of the people around him, he started noticing every minor problem around him. It was almost as if someone was placing all of it before him. He worked on one of these ideas and developed some theories. He was unsure of what he wanted to do with it So he just sent it to an email id which was created within Alpha-Net for submission of such projects by anybody within the organization. He didn't really know what would happen after that, but he sent it anyway.

One fine day, when Ayush was just going through a mundane day at work, around 7 pm, when it was almost about time to shut for the day, he got a call. The person said, "Hi, am I speaking to Ayush?"

Ayush replied, "Yes, Ayush Speaking"

The person on the other side replied, "Hi, I am Jessica, Don's Assistant."

Ayush was clueless, and asked, "Sorry, who? Don?"

With a bit of surprise and hesitation, Jessica replied, "Donald Deck, CEO of Alpha-Net of which you are an employee I believe."

"Ohh yes", Ayush responded while processing this unexpected course of the event.

Jessica added, "Don, I mean Donald Deck, CEO of Alpha-Net, would like to speak to you in an hour. Would you be available?"

Ayush gladly said a yes but was still wary and confused about what was happening.

The call was regarding Ayush's pet project which he had submitted to the central repository at Alpha-Net and had completely forgotten about. Ayush had in theory figured out how feelings could be made tangible. Now it may sound stupid right now as wireless communication was felt of, back then. But what Ayush had done, or at least achieved in theory, was revolutionary for the communications industry. That's what Don wanted to speak to Ayush about.

"Good evening, Ayush," Don greeted.

"Good evening. I mean, good morning for you there in the US," Ayush replied.

Don asked, "How are things there in India."

"Things are good, more routine," Ayush said.

"I'll come straight to the point," Don said. "How did you crack this as the best scientists we have, could not" he added.

After a pause, Don continued, "This is not even your area of expertise. Yes, I know your background. How did you solve this complex issue our scientists have been grappling for years? At least theoretically you have achieved what best of my scientists could not."

Ayush tried to say something but was interrupted by Don, who continued to be in disbelief and amazement at what Ayush had achieved. Don continued to quiz Ayush to understand if he truly was the one behind this breakthrough. After being convinced that Ayush was the one behind the idea, which could open up new possibilities in the field of communication, Don offered Ayush to present his theory to Alpha-Net's board in the US. Ayush was delighted and instantly agreed to Don's request.

Ayush flew the coming week to US and reached Alpha-Net's headquarters, where Don had set the stage for him. Ayush was intimidated by the entire set-up. At Don's request, the entire board comprising 13 people was present for Ayush's presentation. Ayush had a very humble past few years and therefore this kind of attention was quite intimidating.

Ayush started his presentation in front of the entire board of Alpha-Net and in just the first few minutes he left people in the room in a moment of disbelief. This theoretical breakthrough that Ayush could achieve left people divided on how realistic it was to convert the theoretical breakthrough into a technological milestone. It was going to be a game changer for the communications industry, as was wireless telephone back in its days. The presentation was over, and the board was to discuss this in subsequent meetings.

After having dinner with Don later that day, Ayush flew back to India and continued with his routine. A few days later, a call changed his life. The call was from one of Alpha-Net India's board members who called Ayush and told him he was assigned a private research facility with a team of 50 professionals to work on a secret project which will be communicated to him by Don's office directly. He was to start off immediately and report directly to Don's office.

Alpha-Net's board had approved the project that Ayush had been working on. Ayush was back to doing something he wanted to. He was back to making a difference and make himself a name in the tech world.

Chapter 5

A Song That Could Never Make It To An Album?

After a successful launch of Enabler and a brief moment of finding his soul mate in Sheena at the Tech Con US where he had to fill in for Ayush, Ishan came back to India. Given the last-minute change in Ayush's plan to be in New York, Ishan became the face of Sirius in the international market as both the European and the US markets were represented by him. This small luck by chance moment for Ishan set him on a new journey within Sirius. He was roped in as a face for Sirius's future projects as well. Ayush was being sidelined, or so he believed, and their long-term relationship had also gone sour given the changing dynamics at the workplace. Ayush had left Sirius and moved to Alpha-Net Inc.

Everything that was happening in Ishan's life felt like a perfectly crafted story pulled out of a novel, but not so quiet. Ishan was 28 and single. Many would believe that being single was not a bad thing, but Ishan wasn't one of them. Ishan was longing for companionship. The thing was Ishan was a geek, a nerd all his life. At the institute, he focused on studying and at work, he focused on experimenting with new ideas. In the process, he forgot to experiment with life. He worked long hours and never took a vacation or attended any social events. He wanted to change that now; he wanted to be with someone; he wanted to travel the world.

At the same time around, just like any other Indian parent would, Ishan's mom was now asking Ishan to get married. To avoid going through the process of arranged marriage, he joined a dating application to at least experience the hype, if not find his soul mate. As he made his profile and started swiping, to his disbelief the fourth person on his screen was Sheena. Yes, the Sheena from New York. He paused, thought of the good time they had in New York and how sub-consciously, repeatedly, he regretted not asking for her number that night. At this moment, he was not sure if he should swipe right or left. Actually, he was very sure of what he wanted, but the fear of not being reciprocated gave him a second thought. He swiped right anyway as he couldn't add the regret of not swiping right in Mumbai to the regret of not asking her number in New York, which was already eating him up.

Sheena had come back from the US last month after graduating from MIT. She had started working with her dad in his technology company to gain some experience before she could start something of her own. That night when Ishan saw Sheena's profile, Sheena was with her friend she had met after years of being away while studying in the US. They were drinking from the time the sun went down their sight across the sea from the balcony of her friend's house in a posh locality of South Mumbai. Sheena had been single for a while and for fun, Sheena's friend had created a profile for her on the dating application. As Sheena and her friend were swiping, Ishan's profile popped up on the screen. Sheena had memories of their encounter, or rather more than that, from New York and always thought Ishan was a loser to not ask for her number. Sheena paused for a moment as her friend looked at her and said, "He looks good, but his profile is nerdy", and giggled. Sheena's friend swiped right, and it was a match.

Ishan got a notification that sent chills of excitement through him. After a moment of joy, the pressure to send that first message kicked in. He couldn't decide what to send. It wasn't his game. He just sent a 'Hey'.

He waited for a while, and there was no response. By now Sheena and her friend were busy watching a movie, and in the middle of the movie, Sheena's friend was asleep. Sheena took her friend's phone, opened the dating application, and saw few messages, one of which was from Ishan. She replied, "Remember?"

It was about mid-night when Ishan was about to go off to sleep and his phone chimed. He did not hear the notification while wondering in typical mid-night thoughts and was about to sleep. He suddenly remembered that he needs to put an alarm for his morning flight and picked up the phone. There it was, "Remember?" in the notification bar. He was thrilled, excited, and nervous all at the same time. At least, he knew Sheena remembered him.

Ishan instantly replied, "Yes, of course, how can I not remember you!"

Sheena said, "Why? Why so? You didn't seem interested back then…"

"Why would you think that?" Ishan asked.

"Coz you didn't ask me for my number, you just let me go," Sheena confronted.

"I thought you were not interested since you left abruptly without giving me your number," Ishan answered.

Sheena called Ishan a 'looser' after that. With some laughs, giggles, and Sheena pulling Ishan's leg for not being able to ask for her number back in New York, they spoke all night until Ishan had to get ready for his flight to Delhi. Sheena slept after that with a smile on her face and the expectation of something better to come.

When her friend woke up in the morning, she saw Sheena sleeping. She made tea for herself and started checking her phone. Stumbled upon notifications from the dating app on which they made Sheena's profile last night while being drunk, she laughed at it and then deleted the profile and uninstalled the app. Sheena got up later that day with a smile that she put on last night and slightly blushing over last night's conversation with Ishan. Sheena's friend gave her a cup of coffee and asked the reason for her morning smile, which typically used to be a frowning face. Sheena decided to take her friend's phone and drop a text to Ishan with her number to continue the conversation.

She picked up the phone to search for the dating application but couldn't find it. She asked her friend about the same. After knowing that the profile was deleted, she felt sad and had a laugh at her fortune. Sheena could have found Ishan on social media, as she knew everything about him. The same could not be said for Ishan, who only knew her first name. But Sheena decided not to. She was a believer of signs and this unintentional disconnection with Ishan that unfolded was taken by her as the universe signaling her of it not meant to be. No wonder she had been single for a while.

Later that day, when Ishan was taking his flight back to Mumbai, he thought of texting Sheena. He opened the application and realized that Sheena's profile had just disappeared. He thought Sheena wasn't interested, and it was the closure of the story that started in New York. He was disappointed. He really had a feeling it was the beginning of forever. He thought they had a vibe; they connected at a level beyond comprehension. The way they met again on the dating application to continue what started in New York was something he thought was meant to be. But at least this time he wasn't carrying the regret of not trying.

Not knowing what transpired to the disappearance of Sheena from his matches, he went on with his life the next day. His encounters with Sheena were like those mesmerizing songs that never made it to an album. He was so disappointed with the whole episode that he uninstalled the application to shut out any other person. Worried about his singlehood and growing age, his mother started introducing him to girls whose existence was only known to him when he was introduced to them. Sometimes it was 'chachi ke bhatije ke bhai ke bhua ke behen ki beti' or 'bhua ke nanand ke pati ke behen ke bhai ki beti'.

With a perfectly planned career and settled life, except a life partner of his choice, he was living a perfectly happy life—or so he wanted to believe after the experience with Sheena.

One fine day, he saw the post of one of his childhood friend's engagement post on social media. While growing up and making a career, he had lost connection with his childhood friends. Unlike Ishan, most of his friends had either taken up professions like CA or joined their family businesses and moved across borders. If distance didn't, an occupation as diverse as it could get ensured that they lost touch over time. Seeing one of his childhood friends engagement post made him think of reconnecting with them before they are lost again in the new phase of their life. So that's what he did. He reconnected with all of them.

After a few group chats and calls, they decided to meet. While reminiscing the childhood memories and school trips, Ishan casually proposed, "why don't we plan a small trip to the North of India!" It was a proposal that became a plan out of nowhere as everyone agreed instantaneously.

Soon after tickets and hotels were booked, a broad itinerary was put in place, and other arrangements were made. They were all too excited to re-live their childhood memories together, to play pranks on each other, to make fun of each other, to do everything they hadn't done for a while as grown-ups.

They reached Uttarakhand and hired two cars to drive themselves for the next four days of the trip. The last day of the trip was to Auli, a place as serene as it could get layered in snow and offered a panoramic view of the snow cladded Himalayas.

On their way to Auli, one of the cars in which Ishan was traveling broke down. While waiting for the car to get repaired, Ishan, with some of his other friends, decided to go to a near-by café to grab a bite and absorb the scenic beauty of the mountains that the café offered.

As Ishan entered the cafe and looked around, he stood there in disbelief, Sheena was sitting on the extreme end of the cafe, sipping coffee and laughing away with her hair falling over her face.

Ishan froze, mesmerized by Sheena's beauty and in disbelief that he had crossed paths with her again. The girl whom he first met in New York and then on a dating application only to disappear and now sitting right there in front of him sipping a hot cup of coffee far-far away from where he could have possibly been but for this trip. Ishan was mesmerized exactly the way he was mesmerized when he saw Sheena for the first time in New York.

Sheena was there with her group of friends, and they were heading for a 10-day trek to the Himalayas.

For a second Ishan thought of saying 'hi', then he remembered how Sheena had just ghosted him after the long conversation that night, so he paused and decided to walk away. Sheena had no clue Ishan was around until a dog came into the café from nowhere, barking and creating a chaos in which a woman fumbled and drop a cup of coffee on Ishan. By now Sheena had her eyes on Ishan. The owner managed to get the dog out of the café and Sheena walked towards Ishan with a smile and said the same words she messaged on the dating application that night when they matched, "remember?" with that mesmerizing smile that almost hypnotized Ishan.

Ishan kept his calm and pretended to be casual and not give away his feelings for Sheena he had been unknowingly nurturing for as long as he knew Sheena and those feelings had been growing in exile from her.

Ishan casually said, "Ohh yes, Sheena, right?", trying to hide every noticeable thing he wanted to admire from the hair that had grown longer than when he saw her in New York to how "remember?" was the first word she sent on the dating app as well.

Sheena giggled and said, "Yes!"

She asked Ishan if he wanted to go for a walk outside. Ishan just couldn't hold back his excitement and immediately said, "Yes, of course" and they started walking towards the exit. Sheena laughed and pointed at Ishan's t-shirt with coffee spilled all over it. Lucky was Ishan, he was carrying a t-shirt in his car. He changed, and they started walking towards a nearby cliff. Before leaving, Ishan told his friends to carry on and that he would join all of them later. Sheena did the same.

As they walked, there was an awkward silence between the two, like a silence before the storm, a storm of emotions waiting to erupt. After almost 5 minutes of silence, they both abruptly spoke over each other.

"Why did you unmatch?" Ishan uttered softly.

"I am sorry to disappear", Sheena spoke over him.

They smiled at each other; the silence was broken, and it made way for the best day they were both going to have on this trip. Sheena explained to Ishan what all went down when they matched on the dating application and how she regretted not reaching out to him after that. They spoke all day, telling each other everything, their personal and professional goals, their relationships and learnings and what they yearned for. They bonded and spent time getting to know each other over hot 'chai' and 'maggi' and the scenic beauty of the mountains. Their conversations did not seem to end. It was a day well spent; they hired a car from a garage near the cafe and roamed all day. Had lunch together and spent their time on different viewing points. That evening as they were sitting by the edge of a cliff looking at the snow-covered mountain tops as if it's a picture from the postcards, the day that started with an awkward silence in the morning had turned into blissful moments with no words in the evening. Sheena wanted to seize the moment, and she leaned in to kiss Ishan. Sun setting in the background, wind blowing through their hair, the flowing river providing a beautiful background music to their perfect moment. They both wanted time to freeze. They knew they were meant to be together. This time Sheena didn't want anything to mess this up, so she made sure that she gave Ishan her number with a promise to not disappear again. It was the happiest Ishan had ever been. Ishan was taking a flight back home in the morning, so he dropped Sheena off at her hotel and went to his own.

The next day when he landed back in Mumbai, the first thing he did was to text Sheena. He said, "miss you already" but to his dismay the message never got delivered. He didn't give it a thought at that moment, but when he didn't get a response that night he was upset. He waited for the next day and the day after that and every day from then on. For a moment he thought he should call, but then he thought it would be too desperate. But he called anyway and the lady on the other side said, "the number you are trying to call is switched off, please try again later." It had been 4 days since he spent that magical day with Sheena in the mountains. Days became weeks, weeks became months. Every night the last thing he did before going off to sleep was to check if the message to Sheena was delivered. He also tried to search Sheena on social media based on whatever little he knew of her. It seemed Sheena was either a ghost or someone who lived under a rock, as he could not find any trace of her even on social media, in an age where people lived only on social media. Thoughts crossed his mind if Sheena made up everything about her and gave him a number that didn't exist, but his heart was not ready to believe so.

<h1 style="text-align: center">Chapter 6</h1>

If Not You, Someone Like You...

It was summer again. Almost a year to when Ishan bumped into Sheena when his car broke down outside a café while being on a trip to Uttarakhand where Sheena was sitting sipping from a cup of coffee. He would have almost gone unnoticed if it weren't for that accidental fall of coffee on his shirt, quite coincidental isn't it? Ishan was still not ready to give up on Sheena. Over the year a lot of things changed. Ishan got promoted at work and was heading the product development division at Sirius. He had to move to Bangalore to assume his new role. His mom had made him meet several girls from their community, with some of whom he also ended up discussing Sheena as well—of course none of them became anything more than just a date and some of them became friends and one of them became a good friend, Kavya. One thing that didn't change was Ishan's wait for the single tick to become a double tick in the chat-box with Sheena or his search for Sheena on social media.

Kavya and Ishan had started growing pretty close. They started talking regularly, from casually every few weeks to every week and then on a daily basis. Kavya was based out of Mumbai, but she routinely traveled for work to Bangalore, where most of her clients were based. Every time Kavya was in Bangalore they used to visit places and have meals together. Having a sutta break before going off to sleep was a ritual where they shared all that was happening at work and in life. At times, Kavya also stayed over at Ishan's place, and on those days, Kavya used to be a witness to how Ishan thought about Sheena every day before going off to sleep.

One day, when Kavya and Ishan were sitting on the balcony talking about how bitcoins could be the future or how Elon Musk could be an alien or how happy are they in their life sipping whiskey directly from the bottle after starting in glasses, they were lost in the moment.

Ishan was staying on the top floor of a high-rise apartment with a clear view of the stars from the balcony. The cold breeze was flowing through them, making them feel like it was flowing through their soul under the mesmerizing view of the stars. They were sitting on a mattress placed on the floor of the balcony. Kavya snuggled into Ishan's arms. After an initial awkwardness, Ishan was comfortable. As they talked about life, Kavya, out of nowhere, leaned in to kiss Ishan and the awkward kiss ended in seconds. This left them with no choice but to call it a night and Kavya headed back to her hotel room.

Through that night Kavya thought how stupid she was, as it would probably ruin a beautiful friendship they had developed over time and drive Ishan away from her, a friend she had been longing for since eternity. Kavya said to herself, "he isn't over Sheena, you knew it, why would you kiss him, you moron."

Before she finished thinking, the sun had risen, and Ishan called, asking her if she wanted to meet for brunch to which she said "yes", rather exclaimed. Kavya was quite nervous about seeing Ishan for brunch after what had happened last night. "Is Ishan going to cut all ties", her thoughts were killing her. She couldn't wait to meet Ishan but was scared at the same time, imagining what would happen.

She went to the cafe thirty minutes before the time they decided to meet, as she couldn't handle her nerves waiting to know the fate of her relationship with Ishan. As Ishan walked in, the smile on Ishan's face worked like a charm to calm the fire of uncertainties that were flowing through Kavya's veins. They talked, they talked about everything, then they ordered food and they kept talking. They ate the food as it came while they talked. Ishan never mentioned anything about last night. It was like it had never happened. Or maybe the awkwardness from the night was temporary and Ishan could not let go of Kavya, or maybe Ishan also felt the same as Kavya after dusting out the emotions he had for Sheena all this while.

One thing that cannot go unnoticed was that Kavya was a geek. She was as mature as a person in their late twenties can get and as naughty as Ishan would like as a partner. Sounds familiar? Yes, she resembled Sheena. For Ishan, all along, Kavya was unknowingly filling the void that had been created in the absence of Sheena.

Kavya and Ishan started spending more time together. Kavya started staying more often at Ishan's apartment in Bangalore when she was there. More often soon became almost always. It seemed like Ishan had replaced Sheena's face in his mind with Kavya's face and the rest of the person remained the same for him. For Kavya on the other hand, it was probably the end of search for a soul mate. She felt as if Ishan had moved on from Sheena and was finally available for her in true sense.

Though Ishan was less social, he was a social media fanatic, especially on a micro blogging site. He was always amazed at how powerful social media platforms are in the current age. However, he was also wary of misuse of these platforms to defraud people of their hard-earned money. Therefore, as a head of the Product Development division at Sirius, he had initiated a project for early detection of social media posts that can be potential frauds.

Therefore, he was spending a lot of time searching for posts that promised money or other valuables in exchange for personal information. While surfing through the micro-blogging site, he came across an online campaign. A campaign that asked for some of your personal and medical information in exchange for a chance to win 1 crore rupees. There it was. He had found another potential case study which was unique in many ways, He was excited as broader the base data he got; more robust his algorithm would be in flagging fraudsters on social media. As he was going through the kind of information that was asked for, it surprised him. There were questions relating to his blood group, his body structure, his age. Typically, he had only seen scammers asking for personal details to hack your account, but medical records were a bit different. He went ahead and provided some fake information anyway and then waited.

A few days later, he got a call. The lady on the other side of the phone said, "you had filled in your information for a survey and you are one of the lucky winners who could potentially win 1 crore rupees" and asked him to visit a particular address the same day in the evening. He laughed.

He thought his research was successful and his job ends here on collecting data for his algorithm for the project. But given how different this whole process had been so far, he was curious to know what was happening. He discussed all about this with Kavya. After listening to him, Kavya warned him not to go. But he downplayed the whole thing and said it would be harmless. It was more of the adrenaline rush that this had created within him that was driving him there than any human logical senses. He went to the address provided by the lady on the call and reached there on time. As he was waiting in a room in a swanky office of an under-construction building, an old man in an expensive suit and well-groomed hair, with a walk which thudded the sound of a senior executive in every step, approached him.

The man reconfirmed the details Ishan had mentioned on the online portal, which led to his short listing. The man then said, "I have a daughter in a coma for a few years now. She recently gained conscious but urgently needs a bone marrow transplant to be alive. She has rare blood and bone marrow requirement which could not even match with any of our distant relatives, but it does with the information which you provided" After a sigh and tears rolling down his eyes, the man continued, "If you donate bone marrow to my daughter, I'll pay you 1 crore rupees."

Ishan knew it was illegal, but he still felt ashamed on how he had built up hopes of a father whose daughter was ailing and on the brink of death and he would be the one killing the hope of a father by giving false information. He apologized, told the man his part of the story and why he was here. As he was leaving, a picture on the table caught his eyes.

He asked the man, "is this your daughter?"

As the man was trying not to cry muttered, "yes!"

It was Sheena's picture on the table. It was at that moment; Ishan felt elated with happiness. He had found Sheena, the person his soul had been searching for since forever. But in the next moment, the reality hit him. All the things Sheena's dad mentioned to Ishan about his daughter's medical condition flashed through him.

Sheena's dad told him everything about how Sheena met with an accident in Uttarakhand about 3.5 years ago where she fell off a cliff after slipping from the edge while clicking a picture. How she was rescued by the Mountaineers after 7 days of search but only to be in a coma for two years and struggling to stay alive since the time she woke up last year for the want of organ replacements.

Ishan tells Sheena's dad about their history and requests him to let him visit Sheena. For an ailing daughter on the hospital bed for the past 3 years, if this would bring any happiness, her dad did not want to take this away from her even after what Ishan did, faking his medical information which gave Sheena's dad hope of his daughter's recovery.

The same day, Sheena's dad and Ishan went to visit Sheena in the hospital. As Ishan went closer to the room, through the glass window covered with blinds making it difficult to get a peak, Ishan saw Sheena. Her face had healed with no bandages there, but her head was shaved for the recent procedures that were performed. They went into the room, Sheena was sleeping still, she was covered in bandages and other equipment's keeping her body still, the machines were beeping rhythmically. Sheena's dad went closer and woke her up. She laid her eyes on Ishan and had a droplet of tears flowing down her eyes. Sheena couldn't move, she couldn't talk, she couldn't make her eyes roll. But Ishan could see it in her eyes, she wanted to apologise for not keeping the promise, the promise she had made to Ishan of not disappearing. Ishan went ahead and touched Sheena's fingers. They were cold as if there was no blood flowing through them. He didn't know if Sheena could feel it, but he knew Sheena knew he was there.

In that moment, Ishan felt that his never-ending search for Sheena or his need to fill in the void that Sheena left in his life, which he unknowingly wanted to fulfill through the presence of Kavya around him, was finally coming to an end. From that point on, Ishan decided to not let Sheena go out of his sight.

Chapter 7

Destiny or Chance?

"What do you think about this?", the old man at the reception where we were waiting, leaned across the table and looked right into our faces. Seeing us puzzled, he added, "Why do you think Ishan and Sheena kept repelling each other and couldn't be together after crossing paths in oddest of all situations, first in New York where Ishan wasn't even supposed to be present, then on a dating application, something Ishan wasn't cut out for but still tried anyway and then in the hills far, far away from their usual place to be?" The old man looked at our faces which were still trying to comprehend the context of the story and laughed.

He then went on to explain the rules based on which the universe works. He said, "The important things that decide the course of one's life are written in destiny. The other details which do not impact the course of an individual's life are left to chance.

Like you meet a lot of people in your life by chance but only a few become a part of your life in a manner that their life impacts yours' and yours' impact theirs's and that's destiny. Were Sheena and Ishan each other's destiny or just chance or they were something that defied this rule of the universe?"

Before we could react to what he asked, he said in a soft and muffled voice as if he didn't want to admit, "It was none of those, it was just a mistake I made."

From nowhere, a creature walked in. It looked like it was laden with small pieces of cloud, or rather made of it. It looked at us and said "your records have been pulled out but its taking time to calculate the final outcome of your time spent on earth—what you people on earth call 'karmic score', we are short on resources as everyone is busy with the games, you will have to wait here for a little more while" and walked away.

The old man looked at us and said, "Looks like you will be here for a while, why don't you grab some refreshments from the next door."

We insisted on him to tell us what the mistake was that he referred to a while ago and how was it connected to Ishan and Sheena. By now he had left us curious in an already mysterious place we were in.

"A lot of things could have been different in Ishan's life like he would have never come up with an idea of creating Enabler to make the life of a person with hearing and speaking disabilities easier unless Priya Didi had not come into his life or

Priya Didi had not met with an accident resulting in her disabilities. But those things happened as they were the ones to alter the course of Ishan's life and therefore destined to happen. But what was not destined to happen was Ishan's visit to New York and his presentation in the TechCon US and him meeting Sheena for the first time there at the gala dinner in New York."

There was another kid with us who immediately interrupted and said, "Ishan going to New York is therefore by chance?"

The old man instantaneously refuted saying, "That wasn't the case, Ishan going to New York altered the course of his life. So, it can't be by chance."

"It wasn't by destiny or chance that Ishan ended up in New York and met Sheena. It was my mistake, that landed him there," he added.

"You see, the only reason why Ishan was in New York that day is that Ayush had to return to India last minute without attending the TechCon US as his dad had met with an accident. That accident was not supposed to happen that day but for my mistake." After taking a pause at this moment the old man went on to explain.

"I live at another end of this universe. We don't get paid enough to afford a luxurious space closer to our headquarters in your galaxy. Anyway, this sob story of mine is irrelevant. As a caretaker of the earth, my biggest responsibility was to maintain reports on the functioning of the earth for which I randomly had to perform field visits.

The day Ayush's father met with an accident, there was a family day being organized by our organization. I had called my kids too, to show around the place where I worked—it was my first year as a caretaker, so I had a lot to flaunt, including my own cabin from where I operated. Just when the kids arrived, I was going to visit the area around Ayush's house for a field visit. But when the kids arrived, I got excited and hurried to receive them. We have strict protocols, and nobody is let in without being escorted. In that excitement to rush and receive the kids, I left the portal to the earth open, through which I was going to visit Ayush's neighborhood. As the kids entered my room, a jerk to the table pushed a heavy glass globe lying on my desk into the portal on a car which lost control and hit Ayush's dad."

This was all too much for us to process. It felt like the world or rather the whole universe was managed as a multinational organization. The whole concept of life which is being controlled from somewhere else made us question the meaning of our existence and things we do on earth. This was heart-wrenching for us being from Earth as the thought of could have happened with any of us and our lives could have come crashing down like it did for Ayush. The old man saw our faces, which was a testimony of our unpleasant feeling about what had happened.

The old man then added, "It wasn't destiny, it wasn't chance, it was my mistake that led to Ayush's dad's accident and the return of Ayush from the US and events that uncovered after that."

The old man then added, "Once Ayush was back from the US, he rushed to the hospital where his father was battling for his life and with every passing minute the chances of his survival were getting grim. We observed it from the hollow space for a few days but didn't see any improvement. I was feeling miserable about what my negligence had done, and I, therefore, could not let Ayush's dad die on my watch who was bound to live many more years.

I approached my seniors to fix it, but they said, 'Ayush's dad was immaterial in the overall plan for Earth so we as caretakers won't interfere'.

I was heartbroken, disappointed, and felt pathetic about myself and my actions. But I didn't know what to do. I just watched over Ayush's dad's health deteriorating by the day.

With every passing day, pain emanating from the grief of watching Ayush's father die, was unbearable. I couldn't watch it anymore. Therefore, I reached out to the master of the universe over an email. I had heard that master of the universe was experimenting on telepathy with Earth and therefore telepathy booths, that you call a place of worship on earth, were installed everywhere on your land. So, the communication channel was always flooded for the master of universe as the people on earth have been flocking to these telepathy booths or what you call the place of worships to communicate that wants, desires and requests to the master of the universe.

I had never seen the master of the universe, neither did he have a specific name. He was called differently in different universes. For example, you people from earth refer to him as God.

In fact, I have heard a story that years ago, this one time, when the caretaker of earth went rogue and created a nuisance on earth by pitting people of power, leaders of countries habitants of earth created, against each other. The caretaker in fact took control of the people of one part of your world called Germany I think and then controlled the world through that. His powers were taken, but he had a lot of secret knowledge from our organization which made him very powerful. So powerful that no one could possibly stop him on earth or any of the people from our organization.

At that time, the master of the universe personally took matters in own hands. He came down to earth and dropped a couple of balloons with some devastating material called Uraxium, only found in the area of the universe which cannot be accessed by anyone of us but the master and his counselors alone. This put an end to the war by killing the caretaker."

So, as expected, the master of the universe did not respond to my email. I didn't know where he was, so there was no way I could reach out to him. But I couldn't sit back. I had to do something. I decided to get the master's attention anyhow. In desperation, I decided to go and find the Uraxium and use it to threaten to destroy the earth to which I had access to.

Before I even stepped out of my house to achieve what I had thought, the master of the universe appeared in front of me. That was his power, only my thought of doing something so devastating was sensed by him and he just appeared before me. He looked into my eyes and it felt he was speaking to my soul. He then said, 'What you thought of doing would have gotten you into a lot of trouble'. He could see how apologetic I was, and he continued, 'But I see why you did it, so I forgive you'. Before I could say any further, he said, 'To clean up your mistake, I could give you one thing, 'vishamrut', a small portion of it can save lives, but remember one thing, it comes at a cost, cost someone dear will have to pay, and no one can reverse it'. The only thing I was thinking at that point in time was how I wanted to save Ayush's dad's life, so I instantly agreed. The same day, I came down to the hospital with a portion of 'vishamrut' to cure Ayush's dad."

By now we were on the edge of our seats and the curious boy asked, "what's the catch, there is always a catch." The old man had an apologetic smile. "The cost of 'vishamrut' was the life of Ayush's mother. In my attempt to save one life, I took another. That's what made me realize, there are some mistakes that you should not try to fix."

As we were all trying to get over what the old man just said about Ayush's mother, the kid was un-appalled by it, or rather he was more interested in the story than the concept of life and death and so he asked, "If Sheena and Ishan were not destined to be together, then why did they meet again and again and again."

The old man smiled and answered the question. "Ishan was destined to meet his soul mate that day and destiny assumed that Sheena was the one and therefore destiny kept creating opportunities for them to meet."

Then the kid again interrupted and asked, "Ohh, so who was Ishan supposed to meet that day, and what was Ishan's life destined to be like if it weren't for your mistake?"

The old man smiled at the question and said, "let me tell you what was destined to happen with Ishan, Sheena, Ayush, Kavya and everyone else whose lives were significantly impacted by my mistake."

Chapter 8

Sheena's Destiny...

Sheena was at the TechCon US Gala Night and she tried to engage with many people there under the pretext of being a journalist, but the lack of credentials did not really get her any spice that could make her upcoming blog go viral. Disappointed, she went to a nearby bar for drinks. Ravish, who was a Senior Executive at a Silicon Valley based technology start-up, was also at the bar after getting bored at the TechCon.

Seeing a stunning, beautiful girl sitting alone at the bar, Ravish approached her and said, "are you into geeks?"

Already irritated, Sheena gave him a stern look and didn't respond, continuing to enjoy her LIT.

Knowing that Sheena was also at the TechCon he had just come from, Ravish gave it another shot, "I am Ravish, from MacroSoft, I saw you at the Tech-Con, I was bored there, don't know anyone around, can I join you."

Sheena just took her purse from the barstool next to her, indicating a 'yes' or may be an 'I don't care'.

Ravish sat there and ordered a drink for himself. After a few minutes of silence, he said, "Is it generally so hot in here, or it is something or someone special here tonight."

Sheena seemed to not be impressed and chose not to respond. It was Ravish's second failed attempt at striking a conversation and he was full of embarrassment. He just said, "Sorry", got up, picked up his drink, and started walking away.

Just then, Sheena said, "Yes, yes and ummmm, no, it's generally hot in here" and then laughed at Ravish.

Ravish relieved himself of his embarrassment and again took the seat next to Sheena. Ravish was a typical nerd who had always struggled to talk to girls but recently had been exploring this avenue after having spent a considerable part of his life on gadgets.

As the night progressed, they talked, laughed, danced. But not Ravish. He mostly watched, made fun of everyone around in the bar, got really high. When it was time to close the bar, they headed home.

Sheena asked Ravish, "I am staying at a nearby hotel, you want to come over and have some more drinks?"

Ravish wasn't sure, as this was not a situation he had been in before, but he had an idea of what was coming or atleast a perception based on movies that he had seen or stories that he had heard. Ravish said "Yes."

As they walked to Sheena's house, they were both drunk, holding each other, tilting on one side of the pathway to another like a pendulum in vertical and horizontal motion at the same time.

As soon as they reached home, Sheena opened the door and rushed to the bathroom. Ravish invited himself in and made himself comfortable in the absence of any such courtesy from Sheena. As the wait was longer than he expected, he knocked on the bathroom door and heard Sheena murmuring. The door was open, so he unconvincingly went in only to discover that Sheena had passed out on the bathroom floor. Laughing at his own fortune, he picked Sheena up, cleaned her a little, and put her to bed. After ensuring that Sheena was comfortably asleep, he let himself out.

Sheena woke up the next morning with a severe headache and as she really woke up, memories from last night hit her. Her embarrassment level in the morning was as high as she was last night on spirit. She knew she had to contact Ravish to apologise for the previous night, so she looked him up online and it was very easy to find the contact number of a senior executive of a renowned company in the US. She called the number available online, which was Ravish's desk phone.

As Ravish picked up the phone, he said, "Hi, Ravish here, who is this?"

Sheena murmured, "The girl from last night" and

Ravish burst out laughing, which added to Sheena's embarrassment.

"Can you please not do that", Sheena exclaimed.

"Do what?", Ravish giggled.

"I will disconnect if you keep making fun of me, I had a very long day okay, before I met you. I was tired, so passed out, big deal."

Ravish said, "Okay, okay, I won't make fun of you; provided you take me out for dinner tonight."

Sheena said, "I am studying, you are working at Macrosoft. You think I can afford your meals."

Ravish replied, "Can you afford Burger King?"

To which Sheena laughed.

Ravish then said, "that sounds like yesss, perfect, I will pick you up at 7.30."

Ravish was a very polite and articulate person, he was a senior executive at one of the world's largest tech company after all. He struggled to initiate conversations with girls but that wasn't the challenge when he was around Sheena. Somehow Sheena made him very comfortable. Sheena on the other hand was impulsive and adventurous. Though quite the opposite of how Ravish was, Sheena liked Ravish's company and so did Ravish, or may be a little more over a period of time.

So, the story that began with "are you into geeks" went on for a while with dinner dates and movie nights, for almost a year.

That's when Sheena was nearing the completion of her graduation. Sheena had always told Ravish that she was going to move back to India once she would complete her graduation. Ravish, on the other hand, didn't want to leave his settled job in the US and move to India. So, their relationship had come with an expiry date from the very beginning. They were just consuming it as much as they could before it expires. And so, it did.

Sheena came back to India after her graduation and worked with her father's company for a while to gain some experience in the Indian technology industry before venturing out on her own. After taking some experience for about a year with her father's company, Sheena started a technology company of her own that specifically focused on providing services to MSME's.

But before pushing herself into a 24*7 hustle to be an entrepreneur, she wanted to take a break. Therefore, she took a trip to Uttarakhand. During her trip, there were floods in Uttarakhand, and she fell prey to them. She was found after a few days of rescue operations in a state of coma, a state she was always destined to be in.

Chapter 9

Ayush's Plan...

The US TechCon event was attended by senior executives of almost every major company in the US tech industry. Ayush was aspiring to move to the US and join Alpha-Net Inc. a conglomerate of the digital world and had planned to use the day at TechCon to his advantage and make some impressions to achieve his aspirations. He had an excellent presentation by all means and Enabler was not only appreciated for its base technology but also the solution-oriented approach with which it was developed, the thing which the tech industry values the most.

That evening at the gala dinner, Ayush saw Donald Deck, CEO of Alpha-Net Inc. a conglomerate of the digital world. As he approached Don, he was nervous; he knew this was his moment to conquer what he aspired. So, he stood right in front of Don outside the circle of people surrounding him. Ayush was tall enough and his eyes that were desperately trying to make eye contact with Don could hardly go unnoticed.

Don was known for his warm and humble personality. The moment he saw Ayush trying to reach for him, he said, "You are the one who presented that product with ease of communication, right?"

Ayush smiled, nodded and to his surprise, the words that followed from Don made that day the best one of his life.

Don said, "Tonight belongs to you my boy, you have imagined and created something magnificent, wish you had created it being a part of my team."

Just like a kid would feel to be appreciated by their favourite teacher, Ayush was on a different ground after the appreciation from none other than 'the' Donald Deck himself. He wouldn't let the chance slide so he immediately responded, "I have more ideas that you can guide me turn into reality."

Don saw that it just wasn't flattery and leaned towards him, dropped his personal card in the left pocket of Ayush's jacket, and said, "I am available to discuss this further tomorrow, call me."

Ayush was a tech nerd. This move by Don was nothing short of being seduced by someone he always wanted to. With a smile he couldn't hide, he again nodded to say, "Ya-yaa-Yessss."

Waiting for the night to end, Ayush went to his hotel room, where he couldn't sleep the whole night. He spoke to his wife back in India, telling her about the presentation, how he met Don, and how his dream of working with him might just come alive.

The next day he got up and called the number mentioned on the card to schedule an appointment with Don. As the phone was answered, he said, "Hi, this is Ayush, and I wanted to schedule an appointment with Donald Deck for today." After a pause, to not appear as if it's a random caller he added, "I met Don; Donald Deck yesterday at the TechCon event and he had asked me to call."

The voice on the other side said, "You can call me Don, I like to be called that."

Ayush was stunned for a second as he didn't expect that it was Don's direct number. Ayush replied, "Sorry Donald, I mean Don."

Don laughed and said, "Are you free for lunch? I am staying at the Hilton. If you are free, join me for lunch."

Ayush replied, "yes, yes, of course yes."

"Very well then, see you at 12. Just mention your name at the reception and they will guide your way to me," Don said.

Ayush wanted everything to be just perfect. He picked up his suit and changed it 3 times before he went onto make his shoes shine to reflect every ray of light falling on it. The hotel was just 30 minutes away from his place, but he called the cab at 11 to make sure he doesn't reach late. He arrived at the hotel lobby at 11.25 but waited for 30 minutes before approaching the front desk for directions to his lunch scheduled with Don. Sharp at 11.55, he went to the front desk and asked for help. The assistant smiled and personally took him to the 32nd floor of the hotel to a private dining area where Don was already waiting for him to arrive.

Don spoke in a slightly heavy voice, "You are late."

Ayush immediately looked at his watch and it was 12.03. He responded, "ummm...."

To which Don laughs, "I know you have been in the lobby for long time."

Ayush smiled and rubs his palms against each other to kill his brush off his nervousness.

Don added, "Come have a seat, I am famished, what would you like to have?"

That was the beginning of a long, uninterrupted and largely personal conversation.

Don asked Ayush everything about his growing up days and his likes and dislikes. It was nothing like a conversation he expected to have with the CEO of the world's largest technology company. It was like having a conversation with someone you have known all along with no business.

As the lunch was coming closer to its end, Ayush was wary of how to start a conversation about joining Don's team, after all that was on his mind ever since he left Mumbai for the TechCon in the US. Don was an industry veteran and very well knew what Ayush was thinking.

Looking at Ayush, Don said in a weirdly affectionate accent, "pogar kitna longe" and laughed.

This was a phrase Don had learned earlier today, only for this moment. They both laughed for a while on Don's humor but this was nothing short of life changing for Ayush. What Ayush liked more was

Don's personality. How compassionate he was, and it was always something more than work for him. He knew he was in the right place.

He came back to his hotel later that day and was meant to discuss the details of his employment with the hiring team of Alpha-Net after coming back to India later that week. Ayush had already discussed with his family about his aspirations of work abroad, and his wife was fine with it. In fact, Ayush's wife had been wanting to have a kid for a while now but they had been delaying that just to ensure that they don't have to make the big move with a new-born baby to take care of.

Though it was just before dawn back home, Ayush called his wife immediately after leaving from the hotel after lunch with Don, as he could not hold on to his excitement and wanted to share all that happened at lunch with his beloved wife he had been dreaming about this life with. He also told her not to tell his parents, as he wanted to personally speak to them once he was back to India.

Later that week he came back to India after finishing some meetings with distributors in the US market for Enabler. Ayush's trip to the US was as successful as Ishan's trip to Europe. But Ayush had added a layer of personal success for himself too.

The moment he came back, he spoke to his parents about the job offer he was expecting, and they were very supportive of it.

He resumed office next week. That week he also got his call from Alpha-Net with the details of the offer. What he was really expecting was an offer to work with Don and his product development team in the US to research on and develop new products. But he was taken aback with surprise, and a pleasant one, when the offer he received was Country Head —India for Product and Business' Development. He was numb for a moment when he heard the offer and he didn't know how to react to this offer. He asked the team to share the offer details with him and that he would get back to them. What he was wondering was if he was ready to take up such an enormous responsibility and also the fact that he was looking for an opportunity outside of India for a better standard of living and a different life he had been dreaming.

The HR who spoke to Ayush could sense his hesitation and may be, therefore, Don called Ayush the next day to discuss the opportunity and understand his apprehensions. On the call that day, Don heard Ayush out and empathized with his perspective. However, Don said that this was the opportunity they would like to hire him for and gave him a few days to think about it.

After doing a lot of thinking and discussing it with his wife, as settling abroad was a life they had dreamt together and undoing the same was a decision too had to be taken together, Ayush took the job. He joined Alpha-Net as its India Head.

Chapter 10

The Mistake That Was Not Repeated...

After a successful trip to Europe, Ishan returned to Mumbai while Ayush was in New York attending the TechCon and launching Enabler. As Ishan returned to Mumbai at the airport, Ishan did all his paperwork at customs and walked towards the exit from the airport to take a ride home. It was a late-night landing and therefore, Ishan booked an Uber from the airport desk and walked towards the exit. As he started walking, he got a call. He didn't realize that his phone was ringing, as the ringtone was unfamiliar. However, when the phone rang for the second time, he could feel the vibrations in his pocket and so he pulled the phone out of his pocket. Hearing the buzzing ringtone, he felt something was wrong. The second thing that he noticed was that a weird name appeared on the screen which said, 'Adhya Di'. He didn't know any Adhya Di, and he had never saved such a number on his phone, but he answered the phone, anyway.

"Hi, you have my brother's phone," the female voice exclaimed.

Trying to comprehend what she said, Ishan took another look at the phone he was holding, and responded, "What?"

Adhya explained to Ishan that his phone had been exchanged with her brother's phone at the customs desk and they realized only when he booked an Uber and the phone chimed in Ravi's hand, Adhya's younger brother. Ishan laughed at his stupidity and the coincidence of picking up the exact same phone which wasn't his.

Adhya and Ravi, met Ishan at the airport exit to exchange the phone. From a distance when Adhya saw Ishan, she noticed a familiar face. It turns out Adhya was Ishan's classmate from the technology institute where they studied together about 7 years ago. They had interacted during their time at the institute, but not enough to keep in touch after the curriculum was over. After a few minutes of exchanging pleasantries at the airport, they both exchanged numbers and then parted ways.

It is always good to bump into someone you studied with years later so both were happy about the interaction, but Ishan didn't think they were actually going to ever talk again in life, and exchanging numbers was mere courtesy

Ishan had taken an off the next day and most of the inquiries and trade deals that Ishan had started while on his trip to Europe were either closed or could wait a day for Ishan to relax and recover from his jet lag.

As Ishan woke up that afternoon and started checking his phone, he had a text from an unknown number that just said, 'Hey'.

After a little jolt to his mind, he remembered he didn't save the number he got from Adhya yesterday —in his defense; he thought the exchange of numbers was just out of courtesy. He replied "Hi" and then added, "You don't seem to have a jet lag :D"

Adhya replied, "Jet lag is when you feel sleepy and you have taken that away."

No one had ever flirted with Ishan, and this sent him to a zone he had never been. He didn't know how to react, so he just laughed and replied "hahaha."

Ishan knew Adhya from the institute to be a very sincere girl, only focused on studies, and this response was nothing like her. They talked for a while and throughout the conversation, Adhya was flirting with Ishan. Most of the time Ishan reacted with a burst of laughter as he knew nothing about it, and he feared anything that he would say could be outright creepy. So, he rather decided to just play along.

In the middle of the conversation, Adhya sent Ishan a text saying "Sorry, it was my brother all this while talking to you."

Ishan replied, "now it makes sense because I never imagined you to be flirtatious" and that's when the conversation with Adhya began.

On their way back from the airport, Adhya had told her brother that she had a crush on Ishan during her time at the institute. Adhya had never dated anyone so her brother pushed her into it with Ishan and therefore Ravi spoke to Ishan, rather flirted with Ishan on the pretext of being Adhya.

Adhya and Ishan were both single. Over a period of time in the process of making a career, they had little company-most of their friends had already been married, they were terrible at the dating game, and had almost no social life.

After chatting for a few days, they started spending time with each other. But one thing that they both felt while spending time with each other was if it was only because they had no one else, the liked each other's company or was there more to it. But the people who saw them together knew it was real. They were not just spending time with each other, as they had no one else to spend it with. They were naturally spending time with each other, as they liked each other's company.

From going to the adult trampoline park to spending an evening by the sea or just going to a lounge for a drink and hitting the floor dance floor, they had similar choices, and they did this just in each other's company. They had grown fond of each other, or at least each other's company, if these were two different things, anyway.

∞ ∞ ∞

Later that year, they took a trip together to the southern tip of the country, Kanyakumari. It was a 7 days road trip along the western coastline of the country with some enriching life experiences together and serene views throughout. The route included magnificent places like Ganpati Phule, Agonda, Gokarna, Kannur, and Varkala.

They spent evenings looking at the sunset at unexplored beaches where even animals couldn't be found loitering around. At these places it felt like they were savored only for this very moment between them.

The trip, of course, wasn't as simple as it sounds, it was a road trip; it had to be filled with adventures, a word to better describe chaotic encounters with people from different spectrums of the rainbow, especially in a culturally diverse country like India.

One place they visited on their way was Dandeli—heaven for wildlife lovers as its home to Anshi Tiger Reserve well knows for it being abode for the rarest of the rare, black panther. Adhya and Ishan were both wildlife lovers themselves, so they had booked their stay at a campsite for the night and booked a safari in the morning. It was pitch dark in the middle of the forest, the experience either of them didn't have since the time their age had increased in number, height in length and themselves in maturity. It was a small tent style setup, relatively sturdy to be called a tent and had windows through which you could peak into the woods – they had chosen the last tent closest to the woods to add to the experience. It was a long drive for Ishan, and he was naturally tired of it; he went off to sleep early. Adhya was still awake. She picked up a book she had packed with herself for exactly a moment of peace like this and enjoy one thing she loves doing the most, reading.

As the night started getting darker and the moonlight cruising into their tent through the window brighter, Adhya was also moving into a state closer to sleep. But just like a compulsive reader, she wanted to finish that day with a last page turn.

She heard a soft roar, very soft to be alarming, but loud enough to be heard. She thought she was disillusioned in sleep after a tiring day and thought it was the body's sign to go off to sleep. She placed the book on the side table with the marker in it, switched off the light, and pulled up the blanket to sleep. A few seconds later, another roar, louder than the previous one, took her by surprise. This time she knew it wasn't her mind tricking her into these voices. She pulled down the blanket and placed her feet on the ground to see what was outside the window and at that moment a shadow on her tent that looked like a huge four-legged animal, sank her heart out of fear. She decided not to move and wanted to call Ishan, who was in the next tent. A few minutes later whatever it was, had gone and taken the shadow away with it. By this time everyone around the camp site who had heard the voice was out to see what it was.

Ishan was at Adhya's door and wanted to see if she was fine. As soon as she saw Ishan at the door, she jumped on to hug him after the death fear she had just experienced. She asked Ishan to stay with her for the night.

As they couldn't sleep, they just sat by the window and looked into the woods. Suddenly Ishan spotted something moving. It was too dark. Then he saw a cat like animal peeking out from in between the trees. It had golden eyes, and as the moonlight fell on its body; it felt like it glimmered. It was a black panther, a sighting they had heard had not happened for over a decade. It was majestic as it came out of the woods and wandered near the camp site. Ishan and Adhya were mesmerized.

They clung to each other's hands as the Bagheera from Mowgli appeared right in front of them. It yawned, it licked itself, cleaned itself, and sniffed around just like a cat, before it went back into the woods. Adhya didn't let Ishan off her sight because, as mesmerizing as the sight of Bagheera was, Adhya was scared to stay alone after that close encounter.

They woke up closer to each other that morning than they were the night before. It was time for a safari after which they left for Bangalore. They stayed there for a night and continued the journey to Kanyakumari, spending days, nights, and the best times of their life together. On their return journey, they had come as close as they could have gotten. They knew it. They were meant to be together.

After coming back and a few meetings later, they introduced each other to their parents. Adhya's family was quite wealthy and Ishan's family was a little conservative. When Adhya told her parents about Ishan and his family background, they were not happy. Ishan's family was not amongst the top 100 business families of the city, an elite list Adhya's family belonged to. They naturally wanted their daughter to be a part of the same elite list post marriage. On the other side, Ishan's mom had told Ishan to stop meeting Adhya as she did not belong to their community.

Looking at our sad faces, the old man started laughing. He said, "This isn't a movie and I am not telling a fictional story. I picked this up from some of the popular Hindi movies I saw. Most of them had this story it was quite engaging."

What really happened was when Ishan came to meet Adhya's parents at their lavish sea facing home, he was slightly intimidated by the wealth Adhya's parents had created. It was not that Ishan was not well to do, but Ishan had not lived or at least not experienced someone living such an extravagant lifestyle.

After some time of being at Adhya's home and talking to her parents, as intimidated as he was when he first entered the house, he felt as much comforted. Adhya's parents discussed a lot of things about his life plans, future goals, etc.

Then it was time for Adhya to meet Ishan's mom. Ishan told Adhya to come in a saree to impress his mom and made her very nervous by saying how conservative and strict his mom was. Adhya was scared to meet Ishan's mom after this image of her that had been created by Ishan. When Adhya entered the house to meet Ishan's mom wearing a kanjiwaram, they bought while being on a trip to the south; she was astonished to see Ishan's mom flaunting a jeans and a Kurti. What Ishan had done was he told his mom to be dressed like a modern mother-in-law should and Adhya as a conservative daughter-in-law should. As the story unfurled, it was a frenzy at his house and what Ishan had tried to achieve by this was achieved. Ishan's mom and Adhya were friends in a moment. They didn't behave as prospective in-laws would. All three of them sat together and had fun. They made tea and snacks together in the kitchen. Adhya was already a part of Ishan's family in an hour. Ishan and Adhya were thrilled with how things turned out. Now it was time for them to decide on each other.

One fine evening as Ishan took Adhya for a drive, out of nowhere, he asked Adhya, "are you ready?"

Adhya said in a moment as if she was just waiting

for this question, "Yes, I think, are you?"

They laughed it off and spent the evening together as planned. The next day Ishan took Adhya shopping—he said he needed to purchase some formal wear as he was bored with his wardrobe. As they were shopping, they came out and saw people dancing to music. Suddenly Adhya's favorite song started playing and so Adhya looked besides with a smile, hoping to see Ishan but couldn't find him there and seconds later as she looked at the dance group it was Ishan at the center. It was a flash mob proposal Ishan had planned for Adhya. Ishan hated to be a center of attraction more than anything and Adhya endured grandeur, so Ishan had to do this the memorable way. At the end of the performance, Ishan went down on his knees with Adhya's family behind her and Ishan's mom behind him to propose her. Guess what did she say? She said nothing, she just kept crying and nodded.

Shortly after, families started thinking of the wedding. At around the same time, given that Ayush had left to join Alpha-Net almost immediately after coming back from the US a year ago, Ishan was the only person left in Sirius to whom the credit for its recent success be accorded. You could either say he was compensated to stay with Sirius or had earned the title of Head of Product Development looking after all major product development at Sirius. After being communicated this, the next thing that was communicated to Ishan was that to head the Product Development division he had to move to Sirius's Bangalore headquarters.

After the initial happiness of success, the title he was working for all along, reality sunk in. He thought if it made any sense for his relationship with Adhya. He knew she was happy with her job in Mumbai and remotely working from Bangalore would not be an option for her.

Later that night, he went to meet Adhya at her place. He told her about his promotion, and Adhya was ecstatic. Then he told her about the fact that he will have to move to Bangalore to take up the new role. The happiness on Adhya's face slightly faded.

Ishan added, "I haven't said a yes."

To which Adhya responded, "why haven't you, you fool, you should immediately. This is what you have been working for, we will figure things out."

Ishan was a person for whom emotional intimacy was as important as physical intimacy, or so he thought, and therefore he was not sure about a long-distance relationship. But after days of talking to each other and Adhya convincing him to take the job, he said yes. His parents were easy to convince.

He had to move next month and therefore they spent every day until the time comes, together. Adhya moved in with Ishan. They took a week off from work and spent as much time with each other as they could. They binged watched movies and series together that they have been thinking of since forever. Reruns of 'Friends', 'How I Met Your Mother' and Adhya's favorite show 'Crash Landing on You' made them stay up until they cuddled to sleep at dawn. They cooked meals together and also went shopping for Ishan to set-up his new home in Bangalore.

Almost a month later, it was time for Ishan to go, and he left. To surprise Ishan and to help him set-up the house in Bangalore, Adhya had also booked a flight that same night on which Ishan left. When Adhya reached Ishan's house in Bangalore to surprise him, he spurted with emotions and burst out crying as the last few hours at home alone; he was already feeling lonely and seeing Adhya, he couldn't control his emotion.

They spent the next few days setting up Ishan's house in Bangalore and also explore some places in the city where Ishan could spend time while Adhya was not around. She ensured he enrolled to a gym as he loved working out, enrolled to a club nearby to hang out with people and make new friends. After a few days, Adhya had to leave for Mumbai to take up her usual responsibilities and so she left.

They started living their respective lives away from each other while sneaking every moment to be with each other in person or virtually. They travelled to surprise each other over weekends and on special occasions. They ensured that they have dinner together on video calls whenever possible.

It was all great for the first few months. They tried everything to not let the long distance get over them. They even made sure that there was not even one day that they didn't see each other, however busy they may be.

However, over a period of time it started becoming difficult to maintain this. They started using 'snapchat' to keep each other updated with their life's away but that too was dying down. It was not the same as it started. It felt like an obligation.

One-night Adhya was at her office party where she was a little too drunk. She was with her colleagues and they were having a lot of fun. They danced until late into the night. Since it was pretty late and Adhya was drunk, Anirudh offered to drop her home. At the back of the car, as Adhya was leaning on Anirudh to rest, Anirudh mis-understood this and thought she meant to kiss and leaned forward. They were embarrassed and the rest of the ride was full of awkwardness. But she had to tell this to Ishan, who was miles away. She called him the same night to tell him what had happened, but Ishan did not answer. The next day she explained everything to Ishan and after a moment of silence which almost killed Adhya, he laughed and offered to order her a lemonade. Adhya was relieved and at the same time wanted to hug Ishan as tightly as she can as she didn't know how Ishan would react, but the distance between them couldn't let her do that.

This life of theirs continued with the only difference that daily calls became occasional, meals together became difficult to manage, visiting each other every alternate weekend became alternate months. The distance was literally leading to lack of communication and lack of communication into lack of understanding, trust and intimacy and of course an abundance of fights, quarrels and loss of trust. A year had passed by and things weren't how they were, except they were both excelling in their careers. During this difficult phase away from home, Ishan was a little lost. He started pushing himself into work more today than yesterday and, furthermore tomorrow than today. The lack of communication which was the primary cause of all issues was being neglected and, in the process, the crack widened, and distance grew.

After that eventful cab ride with Anirudh, Adhya had handled it maturely and did not let her friendship with Anirudh to be compromised. Also, during the time where her rift with Ishan was increasing, she had spent more time with Anirudh. She always ensured that the social line of friendship was never compromised while with Anirudh, but the line of emotional connection between friendship and something more than that was getting undeniably blurred after a year. Adhya realized it and knew she had to communicate it to Ishan, and she did the same.

Like mature adults realizing it isn't working, they broke up. It was over, though not like it never existed, but they were at peace, Adhya more than Ishan who still had some void after the break-up with

Adhya. Ishan was divulging into work more with every passing day. At the same time Adhya was letting her emotions and feelings towards Anirudh flow as if the floodgates of a dam obstructing them until now were just left open, if not broken, for an unchecked flow.

∞ ∞ ∞

Ishan jumped leaps and bounds in his career. After Ishan's mother got to know about his breakup with Adhya, worried about his singlehood and growing age, his mother started introducing him to girls he was totally not into. Sometimes it was 'chachi ke bhatije ke bhai ke bhua ke behen ki beti' or 'bhua ke nanand ke pati ke behen ke bhai ki beti'. His mom had made him meet several girls from their community, with some of whom he also ended up discussing Adhya as well—of course none of them became anything more than just a date and some of them became friends and one of them became a good friend, Krutika.

It was Ishan's 'fir apni life main uss din Aishwarya aayi' moment from Munnabhai MBBS. They started off as friends. Krutika and Ishan's vibe was on the same wavelength most of the time. They were both introverted but loved each other's company. They loved dancing together at Bollywood beats. Trekking was on top of their travel list all the time. Days past and one important thing that kept them close was physical proximity. Fortunately, Krutika was also based in Bangalore and working with a tech giant.

They spent most evenings together. It was a club or a lounge sipping on long island tea, or sometimes it was trekking in the hilly areas on the outskirts of Bangalore city.

This one evening, Ishan was traveling back from office to home in his car. Just before leaving he had called up Krutika as they had planned to meet for dinner at his place that day. Krutika was closer to Ishan's home, so she said she reached in 10 min.

Just as Krutika was about to reach Ishan's place, she got a call from Ishan. As soon as she answered the call, she said, "I am almost there" and the response stunned her. It wasn't Ishan. Someone on the other side said, "the guy has met with an accident and we are taking him to the hospital, yours was the last dialed number so we called you. Please come to MedCare."

Krutika rushed to the hospital, sobbing on her way. She didn't know what to do. When she reached, she was evidently very panicked and at the reception asked for Ishan's whereabout. As the nurse took him to the room where Ishan was being treated, she rushed in. She saw Ishan covered in some bandages, smiling at her. The doctor said that it was just a minor accident, but Ishan had a concussion and therefore he was unconscious when he got here. Krutika hugged Ishan and said, "I love you." It was in that moment of panic and fear that she realized how important Ishan had become for her. She couldn't hold it back. She had to confess her love for him today because it couldn't stay in anymore. Ishan wasn't shocked, he felt the same and so he said it too. Later that a day, when Krutika took him home, she stayed to take care of him, which he didn't really need. The next day they informed Ishan's mom about the accident and she came down to Bangalore the same day. Seeing Krutika staying with Ishan, his mom implied they were together and asked them when they wanted to get married. Ishan's mom insisted upon meeting Krutika's parents and so things can move in the direction of marriage.

A month later they were engaged and a few months after, married. They were thrilled with each other's existence around to say the least. At work under Ishan's leadership, Sirius was launching one successful product after another. It was virtually as if Ishan had a golden touch. Sirius had decided to move their base to the US's Silicon Valley to gain access to unfettered resources for its onward journey to be part of the world's elite tech companies. Ishan was given the responsibility to set-up operations in the US and he was therefore required to relocate to the US. It meant uprooting life here in India for himself and Krutika. When he informed Krutika about the plans Sirius had for the company and him, Krutika was overjoyed. After a moment of thought, she was also on board, as working in Silicon Valley being a tech professional was a dream job for her as well. With aligned interests, they started planning for the big move. It was to be made quickly as Sirius wanted to start shop already.

After a lot of paperwork Ishan's H1B Visa was in place but for Krutika it was just a dependent Visa as she didn't have an existing job to take up in the US. So, they flew to the US and would figure something out for Krutika while they were there.

Once they reached there, they had to come to the reality of how difficult living in the US could get. The first issue was the accent and the people, they were culturally very different, and they experienced this as soon as they landed. The cab driver who took them from the airport to their residence was very chirpy throughout the trip telling them about the locality they were moving into and how he had come from one of the East Asian countries working here as a cabbie (that's what they call drivers there) for almost a decade and how it changed his life and the life of his family back home. By the end of the trip when they paid cabbie the actual fare, his behavior changed. He was not chirpy anymore and was angry at them for not unloading and vacating the taxi sooner than the minute they paid him the fare. Later they were told that tipping was an important part of the culture and tipping servers and cabbies was not really an option that one could exercise, it was a practice you must follow.

They found themselves surrounded by expatriates from different countries. Ishan had to start quickly so after a day of resting he joined the team on ground who had already started working a month ago. To start with, it was only a sales and marketing team which was led by Ishan and all the product development was happening in India. Krutika, on the other hand, had to first get an Employment Authorization Document to be able to work, which was very difficult in the US.

As days passed and Krutika was not able to work while Ishan was very busy in his own world building up Sirius in the US, loneliness and lack of anyone around with no job to occupy herself with, made her slowly slip into depression.

The moment Ishan saw that coming, he reached out to Senior Management at Sirius and said, "Please figure out a way to get my wife to work in the US, or I am afraid I will have to come back to India." Looking at the progress made in the past 6 months in the US market, Sirius couldn't afford to do that as it would derail their plans, put them back at least 6 months if not more in their overall plans for the big IPO launch on the NYSE later next year and unlock the value in their stock. They pulled up some strings and got her a permit to work in the US and also a job at one of their partner companies.

Just a week later Krutika was out there hustling for success, and her signs of depression started fading away. The more people she interacted with at work, the more she felt liberated from the four corners of the house she was living in with Ishan, who was so busy with work that he couldn't give any time to her. Krutika's work experience in India gave her a lot of leverage over her peers in software development in the US and therefore her growth and progress were faster than her peers. Also, the tier 2 firm's diversity agenda coupled with her phenomenal work made her growth steep within the firm. She was skipping steps on a steep ladder and experiencing growth propelled by the growth of the firm and industry. Shortly after she joined, she was co-heading the product division in 1 year. While on the other side Ishan's attempt to keep Sirius's prospect of breaking into the Silicon Valley and become an Indian Multinational was seeing some aberrations.

This was the point when the relationship between Ishan and Krutika was on the test. Sirius wound up their operations in the US and called him back to India. However, Krutika was thriving at her job. She was growing unfettered on all counts and had established herself as an asset in her organization. Therefore, it made no sense for Krutika to go back to India unsettling everything she had achieved. While not going back to India for Ishan meant quitting Sirius —the company he had literally contributed in building to what it was today. They spoke about it, then again, they did speak about it again and again. The most logical thing for both of them from a career perspective was to not quit. So, they did that. Sirius gave Ishan 1 month to wind up things in the US and come back to India. So, they spent every day until the time comes together. They took a week off from work and spent as much time with each other. They binge watched movies and series together they have been thinking about since forever. Reruns of 'Friends', 'How I Met Your Mother' and Krutika's favorite show 'Crash Landing on You' were making them stay up until they cuddled to sleep. They were cooking meals together and also shopping together.

They didn't know how they will plan family together continents away, but they thought they needed to do this anyways.

The day Ishan had to leave, he walked up to Krutika and said, "Why don't you stop me?"

Krutika said, "Will you stop if I would?"

Ishan then said, "Just say it."

Krutika just hugged him then and Ishan didn't leave that day to take the flight. The mistake he did with Adhya was not repeated.

Though the mistake he did with Adhya was not repeated, Sirius had wound up its operations in the US and by not going back to India, Ishan was jobless.

Krutika's H1B Visa was now sponsored by her company and Ishan's was soon to expire if he was not hired. He reached out to everybody he knew but got no good references until he asked the India head of Alpha Net and his old friend Ayush. With Ayush's reference, Ishan was shortly placed at a senior role in Don's product research and development team in the US.

Chapter 11

Ayush's Purpose...

In his tenure as India head of Alpha-Net, he was set to take Alpha-Net to new heights. To start with, he did not change the administration or the executives; he led the team his predecessor had left. First 6 months he spent understanding the business and various functions and the next 6 months rejigging them. India was a very important market for Alpha-Net and Ayush's performance as the India head was being noticed. In the first 3 years, he increased the sales of Alpha-Net by 6 times to make Alpha-Net one of the largest technology company in India. They launched 36 new products in the Indian market ranging from AI to nano-tech and also some with the touch of Ayush, technologies dedicated to improving the lives of disabled, the vision he carried along from his past job. Over the years, Don had grown very fond of Ayush, the way he was handling the India business of Alpha-Net. He was 3 years later elevated to be the Asia head for Alpha-Net. Don used to regularly visit India and also seek his inputs on global strategies. Some of the products developed under Ayush's leadership were also rolled out by Alpha-Net in the global market, which turned out to be a huge hit. Ayush was growing in stature at Alpha-Net and closeness to Don over the years. Frequent virtual and physical meetings between the two were seen to be fairly common.

In his 6th year at Alpha-Net he could sense a lot of movement. The board of Alpha-Net US used to regularly visit India to meet with him and also to other senior personnel at Alpha-Net. It was slightly uncommon as this kind of interest in the India business was only shown by Don till now and interest from the entire board of Alpha-Net which had a presence in over 100 countries was a little out of place, he thought. But Ayush continued to focus on growing the Asian market.

This one story of his foresight that was widely spoken across Alpha-Net was about how he handled the data breach issue which had led to an investigation on the company, which happened under Ayush's watch. So, at the time of one of the new cloud service launch in the Thai market, there was a complete breach of data and business confidential information of over 1000 customers were at stake. Ayush took matters into his own hand at that very moment. It was his foresight because of which Alpha-Net saved millions in a suit from the government and its customers. Ayush was one of the few people who had seen the data breach as an imminent threat to cloud based system even before it was prevalent. In all cloud services that Alpha-Net provided, they had a real time back up system of all data and every time there was a data breach, the system would automatically corrupt all data, lending it unusable for any purpose. Also, thanks to the real time back system, clients didn't lose any data. An idea which had seen significant resistance from the board of Alpha-Net at that point in time because of high costs associated with it which couldn't be passed on to the customers because of competitiveness in the market had now saved millions of dollars to the company in just one instance.

Soon after, Ayush realized that the frequent visit from the Board was to evaluate his candidature to be at the pinnacle of the group and replace Don. Don, the person he had always looked up to, was being replaced, and he was one of the eligible people.

After a few months process, he heard that someone else was chosen for the job. Ayush was not to replace Don as his successor. Ayush was upset. Ayush was not happy. Ayush was feeling as if he had lost 'the' opportunity. That day he went home and sat with his wife, told her everything and also cried a little. Drank a lot. All things that a normal person would do when they lose a match to the last point or last ball, he did that.

He took some time off for a few days and travelled to their hometown in Himachal with his wife. There, he spent most of his time at his ancestral home. Their neighbors there at whose house he spent most of his childhood, playing and was affectionately called Bunty were still living there. He used to call his neighbor 'Chacha'. Chacha was there at home when they visited, so he also spent a few evenings with him. Chacha was very old and was waiting for his time to bid adieu, at the auspicious ancestral place where he lived most of his life.

Sensing Ayush's plight, Chacha said, "if the scale of what you have already achieved doesn't make you happy, will anything ever?"

This wasn't something extraordinary that he heard but coming from Chacha made Ayush introspect. He was rethinking his entire purpose.

The next day, he came back to Mumbai and resumed office immediately. He drafted a long email for the management of Alpha-Net articulating his journey with the company and also how he had learnt so much from the leadership and enjoyed working in the company and at the end he just wrote, "… with a heavy heart, I quit."

He wrote a separate email to Don showing his gratitude towards Don for all his mentorship. After receiving the email, Don immediately called Ayush and the first words were, "why".

Suspecting Don would think that it was because

of the Group CEO position and therefore, he immediately clarified, "it has nothing to do with a recent change in the leadership, I am just planning on pursuing a career that's slightly offbeat."

Don responded from the other side, "In that case, you have all my good wishes. I am also slightly freed up with lightened responsibilities at Alpha-Net, so let me know if you would need me at any stage."

Ayush was glad to hear that. The biggest name in the tech industry he had been a part of was showing confidence in him as an individual without even knowing what he had in mind. After a long conversation retracing the steps from the past, both rejoiced.

After completing all the formalities at Alpha-Net and passing on the baton to the new chief, none other than the disciple he had trained since he joined Alpha-Net about 6.5 years ago, Ayush started planning his next journey. After his small trip to his hometown where he had an opportunity to introspect his purpose in life, he knew what he wanted to do in life. He started chalking out the plan. He met with investors. He gathered funds. He joined forces with people. He got none other than Don on board.

6 months after he quit Alpha-Net, he was ready to launch what he had dreamt of and what he thought

was the purpose of his life. He started a skill development institute in the remote villages of the country funded by the industry. The reason it got funding was the model on which Ayush had floated the project. It was a very simple idea. He would find bright people from remote parts of the country not based on academics but based on 1-month camps in remote villages of the country. The 1-month camp was funded by CSR funds. The camp was to identify youth who had an instinct to coding. Once such an individual was identified, the individual was sent to a 1 year rigorous training in coding with no formal educational background at the institute set-up in Noida. This education was funded by the tech giants who, on completion of the educational curriculum for a year, would hire such individuals at 50% of the pay of what a professional coder would be hired. The individual being chosen were happy to get a white-collared job with no formal education and a lot more money than what they could ever make staying back in their hometown.

The questions that Ayush faced was that the cost that was being incurred, was it justifying the overall results? We already have so many engineers in the country, why train people in the same skill? What is the turnaround time? To address all these questions, Ayush just had one response, "wait for it to make a difference" and smile.

The project life cycle as explained by Ayush to its investors was this. 1 months camps in 10 districts simultaneously which will go on for 3 months covering 30 districts. On average every camp will have 70-100 adults with little to no formal education. During this one month, all adults would be given vocational training on using computers and in the process, some of them, may be 3-5 in number, would be identified to be potential candidates for a fully sponsored advanced course in computer coding and various computer languages. In other words, 120 people would be available for full training at their institute in Noida. After completing that 1 year of training, these coders would be bound to work at organizations that have funded that training for a period of 1 year at 50% cost at which such organization would hire a coder and therefore, Ayush was using the balance 50% to fund their education. This was giving the company a good name in the market as being socially responsible without any additional spending. Therefore, it seemed like a promising venture for everybody involved.

The first camp was successfully completed and around 80 people were identified for training at the Noida institute. After 1 year of training, only 30 could be said to be good enough to be hired by professional tech companies who funded their education. If you were to see this from a social perspective, the project was a success even if 1 person was hired by tech companies let alone 30. But the moment you think about the viability of the project, the same falls flat on the ground and not viable for the companies. However, given Ayush's standing and Don's backing, companies were willing to give

Ayush another year. Ayush, therefore, continued the same thing for another year. But there was just a minor improvement, not good enough to sustain the project.

As the funding dried, Ayush had to shut down the project. However, in the process, he had visited 60 remote districts of the country, camped over 5000 people and trained almost 200 of them, and placed over 70 people in tech giants who owed him for making their lives turn around. Towards the end of the project, while he was interacting with all these adults with little to no formal education, he realized that these are the people who have the potential to challenge the status quo. There were also closer to the problems faced by rural India, which was the majority, problems currently that were not taken care off by anyone from the start-up ecosystem. That's where he saw an untapped opportunity not just to have some business but also to help to do some social good.

This was his next social venture. Out of the people he had trained, he identified 9 people who could support him in his next venture. The people identified were not necessarily the best coders and most did not necessarily belong to the people who were finally placed after being trained. Ayush had identified people based on their ability to think outside the box, challenge the status quo and become the disruptors. Ayush also made a team of another 12 people who had an IIT background like himself and were experts in product development, software and hardware, some of whom were ex-colleagues from Alpha-Net and Sirius. And of course, despite failure with his first project, Don continued to support him and provided him with his seed capital.

Ayush gave only 1 task to his team, identity problems around you and think of a solution. They were working in teams of 2-3 people trying to create a balance between disruptors and developers. The initial ideas were very basic but Ayush was happy as it was a step in the right direction. 6 months into the project and the results were visible. The team had come up with many ideas worth implementing, and Ayush was already in discussions with many of the organizations to implement those.

Sachin from Maharashtra's satellite town of Navi Mumbai had heard a lot about electric vehicles, but whenever he looked around for charging stations while he was staying in Mumbai after joining the tech company that sponsored his education, he could find none. When he discussed this with his partners from the city, they explained to him how expensive setting up the electric vehicle charging infrastructure was due to cost and labor as everything had to be done from scratch in the city of Mumbai whose public infrastructure was mostly as old as the British era. Then Sachin thought of how when he was a kid in his hometown of Satara there used to be only one electrical outlet in the entire house, supporting all the electrical needs of the house. The reason why he understood it was a single outlet was to reduce the cost of supply to every corner of the house. Then he saw these streetlights in Mumbai which had the entire infrastructure of the electrical supply network already in place. Furthermore, look underneath and you see the car parked and so he thought, why not convert the streetlights into electric vehicle charging stations? This will enable faster roll out as the network was already in place, lesser cost as the network was already in place and broader reach as the network again, was already in place.

The team worked together and crafted the idea into a structured proposal and presented it to various city administrations. The Mumbai city administration or the BMC in collaboration with BEST, which maintained the streetlights in the mainland city, grabbed the idea with both hands and appointed Ayush and his team for implementation. That was the first project they begged, covered a lot in the media for the unorthodox team coming up with such a simple solution to solve a most talked about problem of the 21st Century, to say the least. This simple idea that was going to save municipalities millions of rupees and make the rollout of electric vehicle charging infrastructure possible in a brief span of time, allowed Ayush and his team to be in the limelight.

Another idea that Trupti from Durg, a small town in Jharkhand got was to make roads from plastic bottles. Shilpa from Chinwagaon proposed an idea to have a village level public distribution system to solve the problem of farmers' financial situation.

Ayush and his team's work, which was largely driven by social problems that were being attempted to be solved in the most eco-friendly manner, won them a lot of praise and accolades.

Chapter 12

Ishan's Destiny...

Everything was going great for Ishan and Krutika in the US. Krutika was doing great at her work and Ishan at his. They were both growing at their respective organizations. They were being recognized in the Valley as a power couple, with Krutika having a slight edge over Ishan. At this time, they decided to have a child and start a family. They were both happy and on board. After multiple attempts at conceiving a child, having sex became more of a job than the day job they had. They were both over 30 and they thought it was best to take professional help and like any other couple; they were also suggested IVF. 8.5 months later; they were parents to a beautiful daughter-Shanaya. Life looked perfect in all respects. A life straight out of a cliché Bollywood movie, only lacking some twists and turns. But both of them ensured nothing impacted their perfect life. They both worked and while they were at work, Shanaya was taken care of by the nanny. In fact, early years of Shanaya she was with her nanny most of the time. But as she grew older, she needed more attention from her parents. During this time, on one side Krutika got more involved with work and with her life outside home, Ishan started spending more time at home with Shanaya. Shanaya was 3 and now needed much more time and attention from both her parents as she was understanding what was happening around her and, in her school, which was to start now.

Krutika was almost at the top of the corporate hierarchy. She didn't want to let that go as she thought not giving as much attention as she had given to date would take away all that she had earned so far. It was a mistake in the fabric of society we had built where the perception of women seems to be compromising work when with family, was prevalent. However, what Krutika didn't realize was it was not just her work, but social life she had chosen not to give up was a choice. She continued to have her later night parties with the elite circle of executives. Most days she was either away from home for work or attending social events.

Ishan on the other hand started staying home not just after work but for work. He had opted for work from home for a few days a week from the office which Alpha-Net was readily willing to give. He wanted to cherish every moment of Shanaya's childhood. While Ishan and Shanaya bonded like a father and daughter should seeing Shanaya been taken care of, Krutika didn't feel the need to compromise her own life.

There were days when Ishan would skip work and go out in the parks to play or watch a movie or just a stroll around the streets with Shanaya. Ishan was still a very senior executive at Alpha-Net and at no point did Alpha-Net senior management felt that Ishan was compromising. During this time, Alpha-Net was approached by a magazine that was doing a story on diversity in workplace. The media and communications team at Alpha-Net who had heard stories of how Ishan was taking care of the kid without compromising on the quality of work, recommended the name of a man for the story to stand out as an organization that associated men also with parenting and therefore truly diverse. The media house liked the idea and made it the cover story of their annual edition with a title, 'The Father'. The story went viral. It became the most circulated edition of the magazine in its history in both print and digital space. Ishan became a regular feature at various events hosted by various organizations promoting diversity, as this story was giving a whole new perspective to it. A man with a baby pouch in front like a kangaroo was slowly becoming the icon of diversity within the country and spreading like wildfire in most of the progressive countries.

It was this time around when Alpha-Net's CEO was about to retire, and the board was looking for a replacement. The board had many options, Ayush, their Asia head who was doing phenomenally well for the Asian market. The products developed in Asia were in high demand in the rest of the world the credit of which goes to the product development team in India which was also headed by Ayush. The Group CFO, who had been working with the company for the past 20 years and had been shadowing the CEO, Don, ever since. Therefore, this would allow the smoothest transition of all. And then there was Ishan who was leading Product Development for Consumer Products of Sirius in the US. He had become the favorite of corporate media and could provide a significant uptick to their B2C business given his market presence and coverage.

After much deliberation and consultation with the Board, Alpha-Net announced Ishan to succeed its current CEO. Ishan felt out of the world. He was promised he wouldn't have to compromise on his time with Shanaya if he were to take up this role.

During this total time, Krutika was by Ishan the whole time. She had understood that she had chosen a life, and he had chosen one for himself. Another thing that she had realized was that her daughter was growing up distant from her. She always needed her dad. The pleasure of the outside world was not satisfactory anymore. She wanted more of her daughter than the social life she had. It was the classic state of you want what you don't have. This realization came in for Krutika at the right time as anymore delay would have permanently distanced her from her daughter and with Ishan's new role he would have definitely needed some support, though he was promised nothing would change in terms of his time at home with Shanaya.

It felt like a perfect family. Everything was in place for all of them. A well-settled job for Ishan and Krutika and a loving time with each other and Shanaya. Also, Shanaya had a perfect family to herself to grow up with.

Chapter 13

Can You Plan Your Life, Or Your Life Plans For You?

The old man was expecting some reaction from us. He asked, "What do you think about how my mistake changed Ishan's life from being with Krutika and Shanaya, heading Alpha-Net on one hand and waiting for Sheena and finally finding her in a state of dismay on the other hand?"

The young boy who was probably taking the most interest in understanding the complicated life experiences of people at least twice his age was explaining how Ishan got love and excelled in his career in both situations to imply that destiny can never really be changed by anyone.

Chapter 14

Kavya's Loneliness...

The last person whose story would have been different if it weren't for the old man's mistake, was Kavya. On the day Kavya was to meet with Ishan in that arrange marriage set-up, she was supposed to meet Ravish if she did not meet Ishan. Yes, Ravish who was with Sheena until she decided to move to India to pursue her own venture. But after meeting Ishan, she wanted to take that forward and therefore never met Ravish. Ravish was actually Kavya's journey towards finding her soul mate, whom she could never meet.

After breaking up with Sheena, Ravish spent a few months trying to get over her while immersing himself into work at Macrosoft. Since the relationship with Sheena had always come with an expiry date, moving on from her for Ravish turned out to be manageable or so he thought. After a few months in the US, Ravish came to India to visit his friends and family. While being on a trip to India, Ravish was made to meet a few girls by his relatives to settle down in life and start a family. Ravish was also looking for a companion and that's how he was to meet Kavya.

If it wasn't for the old man's mistake, Ishan would have been with Adhya and then Krutika. Ishan would have never met Kavya and Kavya would have met Ravish and would have got married to him. This is how their story would look like.

Ravish had a very well-established job at Macrosoft in the US which was the primary reason he did not move to India with Sheena. Therefore, after marriage, Kavya moved to the US with Ravish. Given that they were newly wedded, staying alone in a beautiful city with so much to explore and experience, every day felt like a honeymoon for Kavya. Despite having a very hectic work schedule, Ravish was giving Kavya a lot of time, roaming around the city with her, showing her places like he was seeing them too for the first time.

But shortly after, things started getting hazy. Ravish started working more than usual. He didn't have time for Kavya. He used to leave for office before Kavya would wake up and come back at night after dinner. Kavya thought this was a phase that will pass and Ravish will give her time again the way he did. However, the problem Kavya was really facing was she was homesick, especially because Ravish wasn't around.

To divert her mind off all this, Kavya decided to take up a job. As she was a trained dancer, she applied to the school in the neighborhood for teaching any dance form. To her destiny, there was an opening.

As Kavya had done all her schooling in India, the culture in LA was something she was not aware of. Her first day at school as a teacher was no less frightening for her than the first day at a new school for a kid or maybe worst as it was culturally different too in this case.

On the first day at school she was welcomed with some bullying. Some kids had jacked the water tap in a way that when Kavya went to drink water from it, it splashed water all over her. Startled by it when she pushed herself back, she bumped into Mehan, another professor at the school who was teaching Mathematics there.

Mehan was born and brought up in Michigan to Indian origin parents. Later he moved to LA to pursue MA in Mathematics and also teach mathematics to high school students.

"Are you okay?" Mehan asked with a smirk.

Kavya got herself back together and said, "Yes, I am fine, thank you!" and then saw Mehan's face, which had a smirk. That made Kavya furious, and she made a face that said, 'stop annoying me'.

Mehan realized that he was smiling and Kavya isn't happy about it so he said, "I am sorry, the kids here can be notorious at first, but they are nice."

Kavya said, "I can see where the notorious traits come from", in a slightly stern voice and walked away.

Later that day in the professor's room Mehan came up to Kavya and said, "I am sorry for laughing at your peril in the hallway. I am Mehan. I teach Mathematics." With no response from Kavya, he added, "Are you the new dance teacher? I heard you were joining today. Let me know if you need anything. I'll be happy to help and show you around." Kavya just nodded and went on to meet with other teachers in the room.

Kavya was not required to be in the school every day as her dance classes were elective and therefore batches were limited. However, given the environment or the absence of any, at home, made her come to school almost every day.

After the initial encounter with Mehan, Kavya slowly becomes friends with him. Being the only two of Indian origin made it a little more compelling for them to spend time together. Mehan was also married and so was Kavya. But they were spending more time at the school than at home. Did it say something about them? Their relationship with their partners?

With Ravish being unavailable most of the time, Kavya spent more time at school and therefore with Mehan. For Mehan, it worked as an escape from an unhappy married life. They did not realize how soon they had come so close to each other that the lines of friendship were getting blurred. Kavya would soon realize that she liked Mehan and Mehan too had been reciprocating.

Realizing this, Mehan decided to split up with his

wife, and Kavya decided to do the same with Ravish. They started the divorce process and started living together like a happy couple.

The old man then laughed at me and said, "But this didn't happen Mehan. Kavya never met Ravish. She met Ishan and then spent her time with him. She never moved to the US and never met you." Looking at my confused face, the old man said, "Yes, you are 'The Mehan' Kavya was supposed to be with. My mistake left you with your wife who was driving the day you met with an accident and eventually died. You were not supposed to be with your wife that day, Mehan."

Noticing how puzzled I was, the old man added, "Mehan, you were never supposed to die today as you were meant to be with Kavya, not your wife. Your wife would have never driven you to the school in that stormy weather. It was only she who was destined to die today, not you. You were only supposed to be with Kavya. I thought I fixed all my mistakes but this one I missed. I will figure a way out to send you back and if I have to reach out to the master of the universe for it, again, I will."

I was scared because of the previous time the old man tried giving someone his life back, there was a cost, 'vishamrut' for Ayush's dad if you remember, which took away Ayush's mom's life. So, I said, "No I don't want to go back." Sensing my hesitation, he said, "This time, I will figure a different way out. I am senior, I have more powers. I will send you back in a way you would lose nothing you can have your happily ever after with Kavya. I will ensure that you two meet, the way I ensured that Ayush's pet project reaches Don, yes that was me too. You have a day's time, think about it."

So, I have been thinking about this since yesterday now while I wrote all of this down. But I can still not decide if I want to go back to the earth as Mehan. Have you decided what you want to do? The old man gave you an option to join their organization, right? I remember what he said to you, "Your records suggest that you have spent enough time taking roles in various universes, your organizational skills and experience is something the master of the universe would like to use. If you would like to join us in managing the multiverse, you can start now on probation or go back to life as 'Tiakans' living in Universe 12199210. You also have time until tomorrow to think and get back." "By the way, you won't say no to this, as this is your destiny," the old man had added with a smile.

Do you think if I will decide to come back to earth for Kavya, my soul mate I never met?

About The Author

Mehul Jain

Mehul works as consultant by the day and sleeps at night and somewhere in between, he writes. He lives in the city of dreams, Mumbai. He has been writing micro-fiction for a while now and he is also an amateur photographer.

Just like you, he is trying to escape the 9-5 routine (being a consultant it is 9-9 actually) and thought his writing skills could come to his rescue. He can be reached on Instagram (@mehul.j) or Twitter (@mehul_kj). Let him know if he is any good and should continue writing or just get back to his 9-5 routine.